The God File

a novel by

Frank Turner Hollon

MacAdam/Cage
155 Sansome Street, Suite 550
San Francisco, CA 94104
www.macadamcage.com

Library of Congress Cataloging-in-Publication Data

Hollon, Frank Turner, 1963-
    The God File / Frank Turner Hollon.
        p. cm.
    1. Belief and doubt—Fiction. 2. Judicial error—Fiction.
    3. Prisoners—Fiction. I. Title.

PS3608.0494 G63 2002
813'.6—dc21

                                        2001057944

ISBN 1-931561-44-3
Paperback Edition 2003

Manufactured in the United States of America.
10 9 8 7 6 5 4 3 2 1

Book design by Dorothy Carico Smith.

PRAISE FOR THE GOD FILE

"[A] talented and perspicacious wordsmith."
—John Sledge, *The Mobile Register*

"Hollon's novel reads like a dispatch from the far side of human experience, and he has worded it with grace and a deceptively simple eloquence."
—William Gay, author of *The Long Home* and *I Hate to See That Evening Sun Go Down*

"It is simply one of the best books I have ever read."
—Michael Davis, Alabama Booksmith, BookSense 76

"The protagonist touched me and left me thinking long after I finished....It's a fantastic book."
—Susan Swagler, *The Birmingham News*

"Remarkable detail....*The God File* is a genuine novel."
—*The Bloomsbury Review*

"...what we might have hoped for if Raymond Carver had collaborated with Walker Percy—challenging, unsettling, ambitious, oddly beautiful, and well worth your attention."
—*First Draft* (Alabama Writers' Forum)

PRAISE FOR THE GOD FILE

"...compellingly humane....The brief chapters of the book are compulsive reading."

—*The Anniston Star*

"In Frank Turner Hollon's fierce novel, *The God File*, he locks his reader in a damp prison and throws away the key. Bone clear and strong, *The God File* will break your heart and redeem your spirit."

—Barbara Robinette Moss,
author of *Change Me into Zeus's Daughter*

"Wonderful. Frank Turner Hollon is a writer of great power. Thank goodness he is young, because we'll have many more years of his work to look forward to."

—Carolyn Haines, author of *Splintered Bones*

"Frank Turner Hollon writes like he has been around a hundred years, and has seen more than most of us would ever want to. [He] paints a gritty picture of a dark and dirty place...[and] lets Gabriel Black show those of us on the outside a close and thoughtful perspective of the inside."

—Douglas Kelley, author of *The Captain's Wife*

A BookSense 76 hardcover fiction pick and Barnes & Noble Discover Great New Writers selection.

The God File

a novel by

Frank Turner Hollon

MacAdam/Cage

To Lilly — good luck

So you say you believe in God? So you say that you see evidence God exists, and not only does God exist, He cares about you? Spend almost twenty-two years in a maximum security Alabama penitentiary for a murder you didn't commit, and then tell me God exists. I have, and I'm still looking.

They walked my skinny ass through the front door twenty-two years ago. I was in here three months before my mind would let me read, then I started reading everything. Anything with words. Anything. I read a book about a man with cancer. His cancer was cured. He was a doctor with a supportive wife and blue-eyed kids. He wrote about his evidence and proof, both historical and personal, of the existence of God. He wrote about dreams of Jesus and signs that the Lord had cured his cancer. I thought it must be pretty fuckin' easy to see signs of God's existence when you're a rich doctor, with a wonderful wife and children, cured of cancer, sitting around in your country house with your fat dog on the floor by your feet and writing stories about pretty visions. I thought it would really be a test, it would really be worthwhile, to be able to find this evidence in a nasty-ass place like this, with no real freedoms, surrounded everyday with fear, hopelessness, and people who live like rats.

So I started a file. The God file. A cardboard box filled with envelopes and notes and lots of little files, with titles like "suicide," and "Leon," and "letters to Janie." I've been in no hurry. I've gone weeks, months, even years, without adding a new little file, or putting notes in an old one. I've thrown things away, and then tried to remember what I wrote. I've believed and disbelieved a thousand times. The file has gotten fat. Full of scraps of paper, notes and letters. A brown box, kept underneath my bed.

My name is Gabriel Black. I was 25 years old when I first saw Janie, and I remember being afraid. She was beautiful in a strange way. I've always thought of myself as ugly. Dependable, but ugly. She was married and didn't care. She would get so drunk that she actually couldn't recognize me, or anyone else. Black-out, pull-your-hair, fuck-you drunk.

When I met Janie I had no direction, no purpose. She became my purpose, my reason. She wanted things and I wanted her to be happy. Somewhere inside I knew I could accomplish anything, if I only had a reason. Janie was a reason. A living, breathing, everyday reason. A hollow motivation.

I knew the moment I met her that something bad would happen. There would be no way to avoid it. She was wrong for me. I knew I'd find myself in out-of-control situations, and I knew she wouldn't care. She knew I loved her, and she didn't care. She understood the power that lived in her pants but thought it was ridiculous that any living creature would want to get close to that thing, much less be ruled by it.

It seems so stupid now, but I knew the whole thing was wrong when I decided to be with her. I knew before I decided, while I decided, and one minute afterwards. But I decided anyway. And the price I paid came a thousand decisions later, in a shit-hole apartment on a Saturday morning.

The night before the shooting I woke up with a feeling of dread. History held me down. Janie was naked and asleep on the bed. It was hot, and there were no covers. No air-conditioning. A slow ceiling fan turned above the bed. I flipped on the light and spent nearly an hour next to her, watching her. A scar ran down her back from the base of her neck to the top of the crack in her ass. With my index finger I traced the scar. Scars demand our attention. I remember thinking, we are drawn to the scars on the Earth. People don't congregate in wide open cornfields. We flock to the Earth's scars, the beaches where the oceans meet the land, the mountains, and the rivers carving long narrow trenches from top to bottom.

I was restless as hell that whole night. Janie's husband had called the day before. I imagined his fat-wheeled Ford truck driving past the apartment. He was bigger than me. He was unpredictable, and pissed off, and I imagine every night that he slept alone was a reminder of what he'd lost. In my mind I could kick his ass. He looked slow. I felt fast. I spent too much time imagining the confrontation. I know now it was fear which kept my mind so busy, but I wouldn't let Janie see the fear. I was a man. Since the dawn of time men have been killing each other over pussy. We will kill each other faster over pussy than anything else, including food, shelter, even religion.

I was sitting on the couch with no shirt on at 8:30 on Saturday morning when the front door busted open. Janie's husband must have been standing on the other side of that door waiting for the exact moment when he could stand it no more. His shoulder hit the wood, the doorframe splintered, and the little chain-lock popped off. Then he stood there, not knowing what to do next. In that split second I saw the flicker of weakness in his eyes. Maybe he caught a glimpse of his own stupidity, five thousand years of broken glass. I barely had time to stand up.

On the coffee table between us was a pack of cigarettes, an ashtray, yesterday's sports page, a plate of chicken bones, and my full cup of coffee. It was too sweet and after two sips I had let it sit, and it had grown cold.

Janie came out of the bedroom, still naked, with a gun in her hand. A visual image of violence and lust. My eyes slid so easily down her body. There was no time to speak. Before my gaze lifted, she fired twice into his chest. I saw the holes explode open. Her husband fell to his knees. He leaned forward, and his face cracked against the glass of the coffee table, which shattered into a million specks of light. And then it was quiet.

I will never understand all the reasons I did what I did next. Love and honor and loyalty pulled me forward.

I took the gun from her hand and wiped it clean with the shirt that was on the arm of the couch. Holding it in my right hand I pointed the gun at the far wall and fired once to get the smell on my hands.

I looked at Janie, still naked, and said, "I killed him. You were in the bedroom asleep. You heard the shots and came out. Wash your hands, put on your clothes. Someone will be here any second." Janie didn't hesitate.

The problem with making a deal with the devil is that you wake up the next morning with the devil as a business partner. Turns out the gun was stolen. They say the apartment was in the dead man's name. She met with him the day before. Could she have known I would take the blame? Could she have planned it that way? I stole the man's wife. I traced her scar in his bed. I sat on his couch, with no shirt, and drank coffee out of his favorite cup.

Janie gave a statement to the police. I'll never know if she was confused or just evil. She has never come to visit me, ever. My letters sent to her have gone unanswered. The only time I ever saw her again was in the courtroom twenty-two years ago. She sat stone-faced with the angry relatives of her dead husband. My court-appointed attorney was unable to slow the train of justice. Guilty. They call it capital murder. Life in prison without parole.

So does God exist? I set out to collect the evidence, to put together a file, to look for God in the tiny details, the corners of my days in this place, to find out for myself. All I have is time, and this file. I have added to the ideas through the years, like building my own house on a solid foundation, brick by brick.

TABLE OF CONTENTS

TABLE OF CONTENTS

suicide

I think of it everyday. And everyday it thinks of me. It exists as a clear, viable option. I have imagined a million times hanging myself with the bed sheets. But everyday, I choose against it.

I am given the choice to kill myself. I have preserved the idea of suicide as one of my few freedoms, but I cannot do it. Why not? It is this choice against a clear, protected option, every single day, which is proof of the existence of God.

I am Catholic, but I don't think that's the reason. It isn't easy to kill yourself in prison, but that's not the reason. I am afraid of the unknown, but that's not it either. There are thousands of days I would choose the unknown over waking up again in this fucking rat hole.

I don't kill myself because somewhere in my mind I know that the next moment is a gift. The next emotion will hold some joy, even in its disgusting sadness. The smell of another man's shit. A new boy screaming all night long. A maggot churning in the white rice in the cafeteria.

Eddie Mueller is a crazy boy in my cell block. He's twenty-four years old. How he got convicted in the Church of Justice, I don't know, because his crazy ain't fake. You can't fake crazy like Eddie Mueller. One day we were out in the exercise yard. A big black crow came flying over the wall and crashed on the concrete basketball court. He was flapping and flailing all around like his wing was broken.

Eddie Mueller was sitting with his back against the wall twenty yards away. The minute that crow hit the ground Eddie was halfway across the yard. It was the god-damnedest thing I ever saw. He grabbed that crow up and bit off his head. He was biting the neck and crunching the skull bones like a man who hadn't eaten in a month.

The guards didn't know what to do. Is it against the rules to eat a live crow's head? Before they could get it away from him he had blood all over his face with little feathers stuck in his wet red gums. For Eddie Mueller, suicide is no option. God didn't give him the curse of reason. I cannot find any evidence of God in Eddie Mueller, but maybe that's because I'm not allowed inside of his head.

When I see black-and-white photographs in one of the books from the prison library, I am struck by the clarity and depth that we don't see in a color photograph. I think that this must be the reason that most animals are color-blind. They must capture movement exactly. They cannot afford any less. A dulling of the edges, a tick away from precision, and their lives are lost.

Like Eddie Mueller, animals are spared the gift of suicide. They can't see color, and they don't kill themselves. We are allowed to see deep blue skies, blood-red roses, and baseball fields of green. But all around the world, from one end to the other, thousands every day, we slit our wrists, stick guns in our mouths, jump off bridges, and put ourselves to sleep with golden little pills. They say only a coward commits suicide. That's not fair. It's too simple. Only a person without the courage to consider the possibility would try to make it so simple. I am not afraid to hide.

Leon Evers

Some words, strange words, are like people. We pass them in a sentence without a second thought, not knowing or understanding the importance. The word is unusual, long, odd. We would prefer not to take the time to learn its meaning. It doesn't fit neatly into a category, so we skip it, pass it by.

I have time now. I have time to step outside the usual categories. Except for rare situations, I don't need the instant animal recognition. I can learn something from every one of these sons-of-bitches, whether they know it or not.

Leon Evers lost his leg in Vietnam. He left it there. An actual piece of Leon somewhere on the other side of the world.

"I saw it," he says. "One minute I was walkin' through a field, and the next minute I was on the ground. I seen my leg, with the boot still on, ten feet away."

"What happened to it?"

"Hell, I don't know. They took me away. I left my right pointer finger in a factory in Milwaukee. Machine ate it. I wasn't even supposed to be there. Fuckin' machine ate it."

Leon's body parts are scattered in different places the same way most of us leave emotional pieces of ourselves all along the road wherever we go. It may be easier for Leon to visualize, but it's no less devastating for the rest of us.

There should be a way to bring all of our pieces back together at the very end. God should allow us to see ourselves whole, just for a moment, when we've gotten as far as we're going to go.

Leon has been here a long time. Nobody fucks with him. It's an unwritten rule. There are many unwritten rules in prison, and this is one. Don't fuck with Leon. It's almost as if our survival instinct lets us know that somewhere along the line, somewhere serious, we'd have to answer for fuckin' with Leon Evers.

Leon had a stroke in prison. He was standing on his one leg leaning against the basketball pole in the yard. The exploding vessel threw his head back like a bullet, and he fell backwards, cracking his skull on the edge of the concrete. He was in a coma for three weeks. No one from the outside came to visit.

For some reason Leon woke up. I had to tell him about his leg and his finger. I had to tell him he was in prison in Alabama for rape and murder. He took it very well. A lot better than I would have done if I woke up fifty-five years old, in a shit-hole prison, with half my fuckin' body missing, a hole in the back of my head, nowhere to go, nobody who gives a shit whether I live or die, and almost a complete loss of taste. He couldn't taste anything except mustard. Nothing. He put mustard on everything. Bread, beans, muffins, everything.

Leon said, "God gave me mustard. He could've taken away every taste, but He gave me mustard. He gave me a chance to know what I lost. We don't always get that, you know."

Leon changed a lot after his stroke. All of us here try to create some semblance of order in this place. I find myself creating routine, structure. Red beans and rice on

Monday, start reading a new book on Wednesday, push-ups every morning. But Leon Evers has taken this idea to a new level. Now we call him the Fly Man.

I was there when he killed his first fly. We were sitting across the table eating lunch. He reached over and smacked it. I watched him look closely at the dead fly. It was a little one. He wrapped it carefully in a bit of napkin and took it back to his cell.

The Fly Man took out a piece of paper and pencil. He wrote slowly:

February 13th - 12:15 p.m.
Cafeteria
Table #3
Small fly
Left hand kill

That was just the beginning. He has a swatter now. All day long Leon rolls around in his wheelchair looking for flies. He put together a Rolodex which hangs around his neck by a string. He keeps every fly he kills. He documents the date, time, location, and manner of death. It's the only thing that matters. Last year Leon Evers killed 1,827 flies. They fill a little wooden box like wisps of gray cotton. He's made me promise more than once to take care of his collection after he dies. It may sound stupid, but I'm honored to be selected for the job.

When I was ten or eleven years old I went on a deep-sea fishing trip. My dad was a good fisherman. We went out in the Gulf of Mexico twenty miles or so. I'd drop my line when they'd tell me to drop my line. Next to my feet was a bait bag. Cut-up squid, and eel, and cigar minnows inside a clear plastic bag. Stank like what it was, rotten fish. There was a fly around the bag. He must've come with us on the boat. I couldn't imagine he'd be all the way out there, alone with only those little wings to get him back to the beach.

I watched that fly try to find his way into the bag. The smell must have been overwhelming. He'd try one side and then the other. He'd crawl over the top looking for the crease, the opening into paradise. Finally he was inside. He crawled over the squid, wallowed in the juice, ate his fill. Then he tried to leave.

His panic to get out of the bag was ten times the desire to get inside. He flew in the little air space bouncing against the plastic. There was no crease. Where had the hole gone? The wet squid juice on his wings finally weighed him down and he drowned in his supper.

The definition of paradise includes the freedom to leave. Leon Evers left a long time ago. Only God could do that.

smell

I grew up Catholic. White, Catholic, and skinny like a stick. I can remember the smell of my first confession. I must have been seven or eight years old. Scared shitless. Standing in line with older kids, waiting to tell God's Right-Hand-Man about the nasty words and dirty little thoughts hidden behind my freckled face.

I wasn't sure what good it would do, telling Father McAllen all these personal things, but my momma said it was time. And I needed to lift the weight of sin from my thin shoulders. I stepped into the tiny room and closed the door behind me. There was quiet. There was a familiar old wooden smell. The smell of Jesus, and the Virgin Mary, and candles.

I knelt down, crossed myself as if someone were watching, and waited. There was no sound. The anticipation was enormous. Little boy fear. I practiced the words of the confession silently over and over. Billy Kendall's brother had told me the key phrases: I have taken the Lord's name in vain, I have had impure thoughts. "Don't get specific," he said. "Stick to the regular sins. Don't try to get fancy," he said.

I couldn't wait for the window to open. Twice I almost left. I had to pee so bad I actually touched myself. I wondered if Satan had entered my hand and made me touch myself in the house of the Lord. I wondered if anyone saw.

And then the little window slid open. I pissed in my pants.

"Bless me Father, for I have sinned."

The smell of urine filled the little room. I seemed to piss for eternity as I poured my sins out in rehearsed sentences, one after another, in order. I have smelled this day a million times over, sometimes in my dreams.

I heard my father say, "What a waste of goddamned time. What good does it do to apologize over and over for the same sin? It just makes it easier the next time. Great. All you have to do is confess, and the world is right again, screw your neighbor's wife, tell the priest, get it all situated with God, and then screw your neighbor's wife again, start all over, maybe you ought to check with God beforehand. How can you trust a religion where the priest gets so slap-ass drunk he don't know which end is up?"

My father was wrong. My fear of confession kept me awake more than once.

•

I am reminded of my father by another smell. A metallic bipolar smell which seems to seep from people with a certain mental illness. All my life I wondered why my father smelled different from other fathers. I thought it must be his job. But he changed jobs every few weeks, and the smell stayed the same. He wallowed around in the juices of the belly of life.

Carl Anderson smells like my father. He sits cross-legged at the end of my bed and tells me crazy shit.

"I've got a girlfriend."

"Carl, there ain't no girls in here. Where did you find a girlfriend?"

"In the mail," he says.

Carl is small. His fingers are long and thin like the

fingers of a bird. He squints, always, and darts around like a mouse in a maze. And he smells. Like warm shaved metal. Like the taste of tinfoil in your mouth, against your fillings. I close my eyes and smell my daddy in his brown chair every time.

"She sent me a letter. Says she's lonely, needs a man. Says she got my name from the church list. She sent a picture."

"Let me see."

"Hell no, Gabriel Black. You're a pincher."

"What does that mean? What the fuck's a pincher?" Carl ignored me.

"I wrote her back and told her I loved her. Told her I needed a piece of her with me until I get out of this place. She sent me an envelope, full."

Carl pulled a folded envelope from his back pocket. He opened it slowly, squinting down like it was the first time.

"What is it?" I asked.

He held his hands out to me and opened the white envelope. It was full of dark black pubic hair. Enough to fill the palm of a hand.

I noticed the envelope didn't have a stamp or an address. It would never have made it past the openers anyway. Nobody sent it to Carl. Carl collected the envelope full of pubic hair himself, from himself. It was his own insane collection.

"Get that shit outta here, Carl. Get off my bed."

•

Outside in the yard, on the other side of the fence, an old barn cat hangs around sometimes. I can't touch him, but I can usually throw a piece of bologna over the top. Barn cats are lean and loyal. They've got those angry tiger marks and aren't afraid to bite the hand that feeds them. But they're loyal. If you can get one to fall asleep, you can put your face down and smell that smell. The smell of a cat always reminds me of my mother. She loved cats.

On my fifteenth birthday my mother and me sat out on the pier and watched the pelicans. They would float along, fifteen or twenty feet above the water, seeing things we could never see. And then a pelican would stop in midair, rise, and start the plunge towards the surface of the bay water. I wondered, how many times in a row can the pelican afford to be unsuccessful. Ten? Maybe twenty? How much energy does it take to crash into the water, bob to the top, and then spread those giant wings and lift yourself back out of the water and into the sky?

Maybe the twenty-first attempt is the last. If the pelican misses the fish twenty times in a row. Comes up empty. No food. No energy. Maybe after the twenty-first, he can't lift himself up again. He sits in the water and waits to die.

•

On some mornings, early, I can smell ham. I know it isn't real, but it smells real. Along with the smell comes the memory of Chuckie Greenburg. He was the only Jewish kid in our neighborhood. My house was two blocks on the wrong side of the railroad tracks. We got together, me and the boys, after school one day. We waited down at the empty lot for Chuckie to come by on his bicycle.

We had this wild idea. Andy Bailey brought a ham sandwich from home. Chuckie came around the corner. We threw the log in the path. Chuckie's front tire slammed into the log, turned sideways, and Chuckie flew over the handlebars.

Me and Kevin held him down while Andy wedged the sandwich out of the paper bag. Chuckie could see what was happening. Andy shoved the edge of the ham sandwich against the closed lips of the Jewish boy.

"Bite it. Bite it."

"I can't," Chuckie yelled. But we knew he really wanted to taste the ham. We knew better.

"Chew it. Chew it. See. It's good, ain't it?"

•

The smells mix together. Ham, metal, urine, barn cats. But in certain moments, they separate, come apart, and stand alone. I wait for these moments.

letters to Janie (1st letter)

Janie,

I have no idea if you will ever receive this letter. Four years is a long time. You could be anywhere by now. I picture you in an airport. There is no place as lonely as an airport. No one actually lives there. Everyone is waiting to be somewhere else. You are sitting by yourself, with a blue bag at your feet, watching the people go by. The image can make me feel briefly the way I felt every day when I was with you. I have taken the time to pick apart this feeling. At the core is lust. Not a raw lust, but a mixture that left me blind. I spent huge chunks of time waiting at windows for you to arrive. Sometimes you did, sometimes you didn't. Did we ever have a fight?

There are corners of this prison filled with wickedness, but I have learned to read. Reading helps me to avoid bad corners. I have learned words I never knew existed. I have never heard them pronounced, so I have no idea how they sound, but they have meanings which have helped me to understand. I will never need to speak them, so it doesn't matter.

It may not be money, but everyone has a price. They lie to themselves if they don't believe it. There is something so important to each of us that we are willing to compromise. The most moral, honest, religious man in the world will steal to save the life of his mother. The most righteous, holy woman will spread her legs for the devil to ease the pain of her crippled child.

What was so important to you that makes it possible

to watch this happen and do nothing? Does it haunt you at all? Do you wish the truth had been told? Why do you think I stood there with your dead husband at my feet and made a decision to accept blame? I wish you would tell me. I have found no words in any of these books to explain.

The Jews have a saying: "You cannot wash the sin from a family." I have thought about this until my mind is numb. Was my decision an echo from my father, or his father, or just a stray act in a pool of Godforsaken dedication? It seems that we are just hanging on to civility by a thread. With all the social structure mankind has built over centuries and centuries, we are really just one decision away from individual anarchy.

I have waited a long time to write this letter. I waited for the bitterness and anger to find its place. I expect I will either grow stronger or weaker at a steady pace. I expect the direction I go will be the mirror-opposite of your direction. One thing I know, you will forever be in my mind.

Gabriel

fear

Our lives begin with fear. The fear of leaving the womb and squeezing out into the world. Physical squeezing. It is very much the same as our fear of dying. Squeezing out of our bodies and into the unknown. As a fetus, what we know about the world is the same tiny bit of nothing that we know about our adult death. Fear is our first emotion, and our last.

The two most traumatic events in our lives are birth and death. The fear of each is a gift. It heightens our senses. It lifts our consciousness to a level which gives both experiences the priority they deserve. God made sure we are not alone at birth. But at death, there are no such assurances. Maybe He expected or hoped we would be more equipped for the second journey, prepared to look this one in the eye alone.

There is an old man in this place who calls himself John. He has been here a long time, but I have never asked him why. I enjoy our conversations.

"Imagine your life if you weren't afraid. How would it be different if the fear was removed? Some folks are afraid of being alone. Others are afraid of financial insecurity, or public ridicule, commitment, death. How would the decisions in your life have been different if your personal fear was removed from the equation?"

I hadn't thought about life in that way.

"Don't you think fear serves an important purpose?" I asked.

"What purpose?"

"It can't be separated from our survival instinct. Fear

lets us know when we are in danger. Fear keeps us from jumping from high places, or running too fast on a slippery street. It keeps us from taking crazy risks," I answered.

"Yes," John spoke, "the fears of modern civilized man are far removed from the fears that kept us alive when we lived in caves. Now we worry about emotional survival, financial survival, professional survival, and all the other shit we cram into our lives. All the shit we don't have to worry about in here. In here we are reduced to the basic levels of fear. Would you be here if you hadn't been afraid? Afraid of not living up to some crazy fuckin' notion of honor and obligation? Afraid of looking weak in the eyes of a woman who didn't love you or respect you?"

John is an odd-looking man. His face is thin. It seems only a frame for his bulging eyes. He is very clean and sure, calm and deliberate. I wish I knew more about him.

"John, once you start removing the fear, how do you know when to stop? If I remove the fear of pain, or dying, or losing my freedom, then I think I would fit the definition of insane. Isn't that the definition: No boundaries at all?"

•

My father used to tell me stories that weren't true. Until I was seven years old we visited my grandfather's house on the lake regularly. Next to a little wooden pier, there was a leather leash attached to the base of a concrete column.

"Daddy, what is that leash for?" I asked.

There were times that my father was my best friend. As long as I can remember, even now, there was some overhanging sense of pity I had for him. But he could tell a story.

"Well, that leash there goes on the monkey."

I was captivated. "A monkey? What monkey?"

"Your Grandpa has a monkey. A brown and white one. Came from Africa. Got hands just like yours, just smaller."

"Where is the monkey, Daddy? Where is he?"

"Well, he took his little monkey boat across to the other side of the lake."

"He's got a boat?"

"Yep. A little boat. With a little monkey motor on the back. He rides around the lake."

I stood and stared across the water. My eyes looked for anything. I listened for the sound of a little engine.

"When's he comin' back, Daddy?"

"He'll be back this evening."

I was mesmerized. A monkey, in a little boat, somewhere across the lake. Coming back. I waited by the pier. Dad went inside and opened another beer. I could see him up on the porch, sitting in the swing looking out at me.

I waited by the pier until dark. The monkey never came back.

•

The world is divided into warriors and non-warriors. Of course, most of us fall somewhere in the middle, but each of us leans more in one direction than the other. Some folks fret. They worry about themselves, their neighbors, animals, strangers, justice. They worry about how much they worry, about television, homosexuality, obesity, children. There are only brief moments when these people can free themselves of this self-imposed burden of fear.

At the far end of the spectrum are people who don't give a shit about anything. Their decisions are the decisions of boredom, necessity, chance. Roll around in the bed in the morning, never glance at the clock. Reach a hand in the refrigerator past a moldy sandwich to a bottle of beer in the back. Turn their underwear inside out to wear another day. Rather whack off than bother with a woman.

I attended one semester of college. Our assignment in my literature class was to write my own obituary. I thought about it for days. I lay awake at night thinking about it. I finally wrote:

"Gabriel Black died today."

Nothing else seemed important. The teacher didn't understand. Without knowing how I died, or when I died, it was impossible to capture the fear, or lack of fear that God would give to me to make it through the moment.

cancer

The female breast is magic. Women can never understand. It exists alone, disassociated from lust, in the realm of mystery. There's no part of the male body which compares with the female breast. There is nothing magic about my scrotum. Nothing at all. No one really wants to see it, touch it, nestle against it. And I don't blame them. But the female breast is different. It is nourishment to the newborn child. The first symbol of survival, warmth, protection. And the magic is later wrapped in desire, unexplainable, powerful, inseparable from the idea of a woman.

My mother died of breast cancer when I was nineteen. I came home from the Army on emergency leave. She had given me no warning. Maybe she had none. The doctor said, "The fucking cancer is eatin' her up inside." That's just how he said it, "fucking cancer," like he was angry. Like he couldn't understand any more than I could why God would let evil black cells chew up my mother's breast from the inside out and leave her choking up blood on the white sheets of somebody else's bed.

Her name was Ellen. Her face was pretty, but she hadn't much to smile about. Her daddy was an asshole who ran off and left his wife and three daughters when they were just babies. He didn't give any excuse. He didn't have one.

When I finally got to the hospital, my momma was asleep. She didn't wake up. She died before I could tell her I lied for my father when he would tell her we were together at the high school baseball game, or the hamburger place, or down by the river. I don't know why I lied for him. She was the good one, and for some fucked-up reason God took her away and left my daddy roaming around this Earth with nowhere to go. I stayed at my Aunt Edna's house for the funeral. She was a stout church-going lady who married a Baptist preacher. I woke up early one morning and sat alone in the living room in a big chair. It was very quiet, and nothing in the house was out of place, except for me. From the doorway on the other side of the room I saw my Aunt Edna step into the living room, stark naked, and walk over to the shaded window with her back to me. It must have been a regular routine. She opened the blinds enough to see outside and stood for a very long time looking at the morning.

I couldn't move. I couldn't make a sound. Her ass was large and white. I thought, the embarrassment could hang over us for years, at every family gathering, at every wedding and every funeral. Her shape was pear-like. I wondered if she ever owned the curves of a woman. There was nowhere to go. I leaned back ever so slowly, rested my head against the chair, and closed my eyes. I figured if she saw me before she left the room, the belief that I was sound asleep could save us both. I peeked. After a few minutes my Aunt Edna turned around and stood frozen. She squinted her old eyes and saw me asleep in the chair. Her breasts hung long and meaty, nipples pointed downwards as she tiptoed from the room.

•

I don't understand cancer. It seems to be a form of cannibalism. We eat ourselves. For some unknown reason we are at peace with this powerful misunderstanding. They put crosses on the sides of highways where people die in car wrecks. They decorate these crosses with flowers and wreaths. Nobody put a cross in the hospital bed where cancer killed my momma. Nobody put a cross in the grocery store, or the beauty parlor, or wherever it was that the first little cancer cell appeared in the chest of my mother, not far from the nipple I suckled, and desired, and tried to forget. Are we so afraid of the cancer beast that we let it take who it wishes, as long as it leaves the rest of us alone? Or are we simply baffled by the mystery of this cancer, this evil we can't understand, and feel abandoned by God for letting it do what it wants? The honeybee sacrifices its life for the sting. The wasp lives to sting and sting again, as it wishes.

My Aunt Edna sat by the bed of my mother for her last four days. She said they talked like sisters do. I wanted to know what my mother said.

"Your mother was in and out, Gabe. She knew what was happening, but they had her on medication. She knew you were coming to see her. I told her so, and I told her you called. I told her we haven't been able to find your brother."

"Did she say anything about my dad?"

"One time, when she was delirious, she seemed to be talking to your father. She was telling him to be quiet because the children were asleep. She was telling him to finish his biscuits. It's funny how little tiny pieces of our lives get stuck somewhere and come out at the end. I guess we don't ever know what's gonna be important."

"Was she afraid to die?"

"I don't think so, Gabe."

"I wish I could have made it here to talk to her. I wanted to hear her voice. She had that easy, calm voice. Sad and not sad. Kinda like a song. I wanted to hear it one more time."

"She knew you were coming, Gabe. The day before she died, she told me she knew you were coming. She said she could tell for sure because she'd seen the butterflies. She said she'd always see the butterflies right before you come home. She told me that."

Momma never had to see me in shackles. She never had to sit in the courtroom, torn between the love of her child and hatred. She never had to see me go to prison, or look at my face on the other side of the steel bars, or lie awake at night in her bed and wonder what unspeakable thing was happening to her boy in a prison-house shower.

letters to Janie (2nd letter)

Janie,

I never heard from you after the letter I sent three years ago. As long as it never comes back, I will believe you got it. In my mind I watched you sit on a porch swing and open the envelope. The image always has the same details: a big orange cat on the porch rail, a breeze through your hair, the swing moves slow side to side. I can never really see the expression on your face as you read the letter. The cat stretches, or the breeze blows, and I am distracted. But there is always more time, plenty of time in here to recapture the scene. I look forward to the chance to see you again.

I don't wonder anymore whether you will come forward to tell the truth about what happened. It wouldn't make a difference anyway. I do wonder, did you select me? There were other men in that bar on that certain night. What did you see in me from across the room? I wish you had met my mother. I could have learned more from her eyes than from my own. Did you know your husband was coming over that morning? Did you have the gun loaded and ready? Were you thinking about it while we were in bed? Why didn't you just shoot me, too, standing next to the couch, on the other side of the coffee table from the man on his knees?

What was the trade-off? What were you willing to give? What do you have now? I'm curious. Who lives in that house with the big white swing on the porch? Who handed you my envelope? Was there a question: "Who is Gabriel Black?" We should have gotten to know each other before we fucked in the bathroom at the Texaco. I should have known your middle name. You should have known I like ice cream. Instead, we were stuck together like two dogs in the yard, in a gas station bathroom on a Saturday night. I can see the side of your face in the mirror. Your eyes are shut tight, like it hurts. I can't stop. I want to, but I can't.

I thought I learned discipline in the Army. I learned nothing compared to the lessons of discipline I have learned here. I found a book about running a marathon. I traced and charted the steps in the exercise yard. I calculated in minutes, and then seconds, and finally in portions of seconds, too small to matter. When the door would swing open into the exercise yard I would take off, in my boots, barefooted, whatever they would let me do. I would go back to my cell, run in place, count the steps, add up the miles, figure out the pace, and imagine running the New York City Marathon on a cool November morning. It ends in Central Park. You could knock down these walls, burn this building, blast these fucking guards to the edge of the universe. The prison remains. It is a prison of my obligations, loyalties, responsibilities. I am held by them like chains, and ropes, and barking dogs at the gate.

I never felt jealousy until you. I wasn't even sure what people were talking about when they spoke of being in a "jealous rage," or "blinded by jealousy." I probably would have killed your husband myself, eventually. I couldn't have lived with the idea of him inside you, with your eyes squinted, giving yourself away to that fat son-of-a-bitch. And if I had waited, your next man would have felt the same way about me.

Drop me a card sometime.

Gabe

my father

He was like me, not a big man. A mechanic. There was always grease under his nails. I learned how to fix a car from him. "You gotta understand a car before you can fix it," Daddy would say, "You ain't never gonna outsmart anybody, boy. You come from a family of scavengers. Anything you can think of, it's been thought about before. Believe me. Ain't nothin' new."

There must have been a time in his life when he thought he could change the world. He was the first one in his family to go to college. They put together enough money to send him to the University of Alabama. Daddy would tell stories about trying to get into the fraternity.

"They brought a big block a ice, sat it down on the back porch. Ten feet away they put a bucket. There were eight of us. We were the kids they knew would never make it. We were the kids they could piss around with.

"Jar a green olives was poured out on top of the block a ice. They made me go first. Drop my pants. Sit down on that block a ice. Try to pick up one of them olives with my ass cheeks, carry it across the porch and drop it in the bucket. I had fifteen minutes to get as many of them olives as I could get, fifteen minutes sittin' on a block a ice, my ass got so cold I couldn't feel nothin'. Couldn't tell whether or not a goddamned olive was wedged up in there or not. I'd waddle across the porch, straddle the bucket, shake my ass to see if anything would fall. Felt like a fuckin' idiot, packed up my shit and went home. Beat all hell out of one of those frat boys three weeks later at a bar on the strip."

At some point in time I found out my daddy failed out of school his first year. He didn't go back, because they wouldn't let him. Somewhere in the back of his mind he wanted me and my big brother to fail. He got his wish, at least partly.

•

The first time I was raped in this place I thought about my daddy. I can't explain why. I don't want to know. I had only been here a week. Had no idea what it takes to survive. I was small, and walked with a limp from the time I broke my leg when I was a boy. I was selected for my weakness, like animals separate the herd. It ain't got shit to do with pretty.

There were three of them. Strong. Thought it was funny. I fought like a dog, bit, scratched, felt the punch shatter my ribs and suck the breath from my lungs. Felt my pants pulled down to my ankles, and thought about my daddy. Sittin' there, on that "block a ice," being laughed at, knowing it was for nothin'.

When it happened the second time I was ready. I fought until they thought I was done fighting, and then cut the man's ball sack from one side to the other with a piece of a razor. It was the last time they tried. The risk and the reward were no longer equal. You should have seen his face that split second from the time he saw what I had done until the pain shot up his backbone.

•

When I was six years old my daddy took me deer hunting. We sat out in the woods for hours, listening, cold. Real cold. My daddy got permission from the farmer down the road, Ed Creech, to hunt his land.

Daddy had good luck before in Mr. Creech's woods.

There was a sound. A twig snapped. Maybe on the ground. Daddy lifted his head. The rifle rose to his shoulder. There was quiet, and then the explosion of a shot. My ears rang. He ran, and I ran after him, through the woods, with the cold air in and out. And then he stopped, dead still, on the ground, in front of us, was a donkey. Shot, bloody, still-moving, donkey.

My father cussed a streak like I never heard. I thought he might kill us all. It took fifteen minutes before he could talk normal. I cried the whole time, not knowing why, why that donkey kicked around on the ground.

My daddy walked over, held the rifle against its head, put a hand over his own face, and blew half that donkey's head off.

He looked at me. "Boy, this is Mr. Creech's donkey. I killed the man's donkey. If he finds out, we'll never hunt out here again. He's liable to have my ass arrested."

We dragged that donkey by its hind legs all the way back to the truck. My father used all his strength to lift the dead beast into the bed of the truck. We drove down to the river and buried the animal in the soft dirt not far from the water.

"You ever tell anybody, anybody, about what happened today, I swear to God I will beat you until you can't see."

•

A couple of years later, me and my brother were listening at the top of the stairs to my daddy and his friends playing poker in the living room. They cussed like sailors and smoked cigars across the room from my mother's statue of the Virgin Mary on the mantel above the fireplace. I could hear the sound of glass on glass as Daddy would pour whiskey.

I listened to him tell the story about the donkey, with the perfect rhythm of the whiskey, like only my daddy could. The men listened to every word, laughed when my daddy wanted them to laugh. My brother turned from the stair below to watch my face. The men around the table could see that donkey being drug back to the truck as clear as if they had been there themselves. They could see that little boy, frightened out of his mind, helping his daddy bury Mr. Creech's donkey in the river bed.

I don't know if my father is still alive. He came to visit a few times and wrote me a letter, but I haven't heard from him in a lot of years. He was a lazy drunk, who always looked for the easy way out, and lied to my momma. But he could tell a story. I swear to God, when he was on the topside of his downswing, he could tell a story. And while he was telling it, it was the only thing that mattered. Sometimes God hides Himself in the cracks between the words.

suicide continued

There is no way for me to really capture the hopelessness of this place in the notes I keep. There is no way to describe the repetition of each day and the slow surrender. It would be page after empty page, with maybe a word or a few words clumped together every now and then. There is no way to dig a hole in the page for the reader to step inside, into quicksand in the pitch-black dark. I'm not even sure I would want anyone else to feel it.

There is something soothing about the Catholic religion. To someone on the outside, the rituals and chants probably seem crazy. But to us, it would be crazy not to have them. "Ceremonies of security," John calls them.

The church was a part of my life as a boy. It was very important to my mother. Her strength to survive came from the church. It wasn't a physical strength, or mental, but came from someplace an animal cannot reach. I felt a debt to believe, for the sake of my mother.

The Catholic church taught us to believe that God can never forgive a person for committing suicide. I do not believe this is true. It seems to me that if anyone needed God, needed forgiveness, needed to be held, it would be the person who cannot find the strength to make it in this life another minute. How can the all-knowing, the all-loving, the all-forgiving God turn his back on his weakest child? They say that the greatest sadness is the loss of a child.

•

When I was eleven years old my father gave me a bow and arrow. It was a long curved wooden bow with a tight string. The arrows all had tips sharp as razors. My father wanted me to learn to love to hunt. He thought it would make me into a man.

A kid named Jeff lived across the street. His head was too big and other kids in the neighborhood didn't like him. I walked with a limp. Jeff was drawn to me.

The only thing I gave a shit about most of the time was my dog, Banjo. Banjo was a mutt. Smartest damn dog I ever knew. He could catch squirrels. Sneak up really slow, inch by inch. Would squint his eyes like it made it harder for the squirrels to see him. That stupid-ass squirrel would be chewing on a nut one second and the next second Banjo would snap his neck in a quick shake. He'd walk around all day showing that squirrel to anyone who would look.

We were standing in the front yard. Jeff came across the street. He asked to see the bow and arrow. He ran his hand from the top of the wooden bow to the bottom. He plucked the string and felt the sharp tip of the arrow with his finger. He put the arrow in place against the string and pulled it tight. There was no warning. He turned the arrow up to the sky, pulled back as tight as it would go, and let loose. The arrow flew straight up in the air.

I watched it go like it wasn't real. There was no way to guess where that arrow would come down, razor first. I ran to the screen door screaming at Jeff. He just stood there, frozen. I imagine the arrow reached as high as it would go, turned over, and headed back down to earth. I got to the screen door and turned around just in time to see the arrow go through the back of my dog and out his belly. He stood there for a split second, an arrow through his body, with no understanding of the pain, or the arrow, or the idiotic motherfucker standing in my front yard with a bow in his hand staring up into the sun with his arms stretched out waiting for God knows what.

From that day on, every time I saw that fucking idiot, I beat him until my hands hurt. I beat him so bad once they took me to the juvenile home. I broke two fingers on my right hand. Jeff's parents moved away and took him somewhere else. I thought I saw him here once, but it wasn't him.

One day, when I was fifteen years old, my father didn't come home from work. They found his car on the side of the dirt road he traveled everyday from work to home in the afternoon. The engine was still running. The radio was on, and my daddy's lunch pail sat on the front seat with a half-eaten sandwich inside.

They found him in the middle of the empty farm field two hundred yards from the car. My father was driving home on a regular Tuesday afternoon. He pulled his car over to the side of the road, grabbed his pistol from under the seat, and walked out into an empty plowed field. He shot himself in the head. But as usual he screwed it all up. He must have been walking when he lifted the gun to his temple. He must have tripped or stumbled, I'll never know, but the bullet took off half his ear and cut across his skull. When he came home he looked like a mummy. He left no note, no letter, nothing. After the policeman told us what happened, my mother sat me and my brother down in the living room. She told us we could never talk about what Daddy did. As far as she was concerned, it never happened. As far as she was concerned, God refused to let Daddy kill himself because if he killed himself Daddy would lose his place in Heaven.

laughter

There are people in this place who go for days without laughing. They go for days without smiling. And then there are people like Carl. I've seen Carl laugh so hard, for hours, I thought he would suffocate. I put a check-mark next to the "laughter" file. It is clear evidence of God. What else could it be?

I sat around the table with John, Leon Evers, and Carl.

"What's the most fucked-up job you ever had?"

Carl raised his hand like the kid in class. He didn't wait to be selected.

"I drove a bread truck."

"What's fucked-up about that?"

"Nothin'," Carl said, "except one day, I was deliverin' bread in a neighborhood on Tunstall Road. I took a turn too fast. The back doors of the truck swung open, and the bread trays slid out onto the road."

Carl laughed to himself. He stared down when he told the story like he was watching himself on television.

"When I seen in the mirror what happened, I stopped the truck and backed up. There must've been fifty loaves of bread in the road. All over the damned place.

"I got out of the truck and started to grab up the bread, and then I saw this dog, a little white pug-faced dog. He come up and smelled on a loaf of bread. Started to drag it off. I said, 'Hey, you little shithead, drop the bread.'

"He run off. And then there was another dog. A big

black one. And behind him was a collie, and two dirty poodles, and then a fuckin' weenie dog."

I turned my head to laugh. You can never tell when Carl might get offended. I could imagine that crazy little man chasing dogs in the road.

Carl looked up. "They were everywhere. Bustin' open plastic wrappers. It was like an ambush. Like they was waitin' for my truck to go by. Little shitheads."

Carl's mood changed.

"I got fired. They made me pay for all the bread the dogs got."

Carl hesitated and said, "I bought all them dogs lunch."

Leon Evers let out a little laugh. Carl looked across the table at each of us. It was some mental survey. And then he laughed, too. We all did. First small, and then full.

After a few minutes John raised his hand.

"I worked in a funeral home. When a body would come in, we used to get it ready for the funeral. We'd tilt the table, shove a tube in the neck, and drain all the blood to the floor and down a hole."

Carl was curious. He asked, "What do you do with the eyeballs?"

"You pop 'em. Fill the holes so the eyelids don't sink in."

Carl made a face. He asked, "What's the weirdest thing you ever saw on a dead body?"

John thought a minute. I wondered what things he remembered and decided didn't qualify as the weirdest.

John smiled, "I had a man brought in, about eighty

years old. He had a tattoo on his dick. I had to stretch it out to see what it said, longways, it said 'Honey Stick'."

Leon Evers laughed again.

"A year later they brought in his wife. Eighty-year-old blue-haired woman. Right above her cooter she had a tattoo that said 'Honey Pot'."

Leon said, "I'll be damned. 'Honey Stick' and 'Honey Pot'. I'll be damned."

"That's a true story," John said, "I couldn't help thinking how they probably got those tattoos some wild night together, and through the years, when the wildness and passion had slipped away, how strange it must have been for that man to read 'Honey Stick' written along his shaft every time he took a piss.

"I'm sure their children, grandchildren, best friends never knew it. But the funeral man sees everything. I put a penny in their asses for luck."

"Your turn, Leon."

"I don't remember."

"Sure you do. Try to think. What did you do before you came here?"

Leon said, "I crapped at the Alamo."

I laughed out loud. John did, too. Carl looked confused. He said, "That ain't no job. How's that a job?"

Leon wasn't sure. He said, "I did have a job once. Worked at a cracker factory in Milwaukee. Millions of crackers, saltines, come through that factory, on a conveyor belt. I was a salter. A cracker salter. Sat on a stool, shook salt on crackers while they went by."

Carl surveyed our faces again. He needed to make sure this wasn't a trick on him. He needed to make sure we weren't all in on something he didn't know.

Carl said, "Cracker salter? What the hell kinda job is that? That ain't hard."

Leon seemed offended. "Hell it ain't. You ever tried to get grains of salt to stay on a cracker? Most of the time they roll right off. Roll off the side of the cracker."

Carl wrinkled up his forehead. He thought about it for a little while.

Leon said, "I finally figured out the salt would stick a lot better if I licked the cracker first. After a big lick, the salt would stay on better."

Carl slapped his knee and spun around. "That's the craziest shit I ever heard. You can't lick no cracker every time you sprinkle salt."

When Carl was looking away, Leon winked at me. Sitting around that table I forgot I was in the joint. We all did. We could've been kids at the ballpark. A few minutes of solid, real laughter.

Janie,

I know it sounds weird, but when we were together, I can remember specific times when I would actually stop and try to gather every piece of the moment. There was always a feeling that later I would need to remember. It's harder now to imagine your face. I don't have a picture to remind me. Some nights I can't get it right, and it takes me a long time for you to come into focus. Your eyes are the hardest for me to see again.

It's strange, when a man is alone, without a woman, for weeks and years, the sexual memories eventually become the strongest. They are clear and exist like tiny movies in my mind. I can barely remember your face, but I can remember every freckle and line on your back. The night at Paul's house. The lights were on in the bedroom. You rolled over on your stomach and gave yourself to me completely. Why would God let me remember this, and not let me remember holding hands with you, or conversations at the kitchen table, or a day at the beach? Why would He allow me this memory, alone in a prison of men?

Gabriel

dreams

I am tangled in dreams. The same dreams. I have had them for as long as I can remember. When I am in them, they are real. Even though I have been there so many times before, it always feels the same. I always stop in the same spot.

Dream #1

From a high place, maybe a building, I look down at a city street. I am too high to see faces, but low enough to see the colors of people's clothes and a cat in the arms of a lady waiting on the sidewalk for her child to come home from school.

A big yellow school bus comes around the corner of the block. I watch it slowly approach the lady and see the red lights begin to flash as it slows. The bus comes to a stop, and the door swings open on the far side away from my view. I can see children inside the bus crawling from their seats and forming a line in the aisle. They step off the bus one by one and in a straight line move in front of the bus and begin to cross the street.

At the end of the block I can see a blue car fly around the corner. It's going too fast. I can't see the driver. The blue car gets closer and closer to the children. It's going too fast. The car swerves around the bus into the middle of the street. The heads of the children turn at the same time to see the blue car. It's too late.

At the moment the front bumper of the car crashes into the line of children, my view changes. I am behind the wheel. The first thing I see is the face of a little girl against the windshield. Her book bag flies slowly through the air and lands in the street.

The dream is over.

Dream #2

I am a young man, maybe fourteen years old. I've lived my whole life in a coastal town. I am most comfortable on a sailboat alone. My father, and his father, have taught me the sea.

Down the beach from the harbor there is a rocky point. The rocks extend from the shore out into the rough current. All my life I have been told the stories of ships and men crushed and lost at the point. The currents suck anything afloat into the jagged rocks. Just below the surface there is danger which can't be seen. I am drawn.

At a certain time, on a certain day, I climb into my boat and steer towards the point. On the first pass I keep a safe distance, the distance my daddy taught me. I circle back and pass again and again, each time closer to the rocks, each time a few feet nearer the current which pulls with its unforgiving force.

My eyes narrow in the mist exploding from the rocks. I cannot feel a smile on my face, but it is there. With each pass, each additional risk, I become more calm. The contrast between the inside and the outside widens. And then, in an instant, I have gone too far.

I close my eyes. The dream ends.

Dream #3

Since I came to prison, I have had another recurring

dream about sailboats. I am alone, night watch, high above deck in a crow's nest on the mast of a big ship. It is very quiet with a cool breeze. The reflection from the moon gives the only light. The black ocean is all there is to see.

As morning comes, and the first light of the day glows, a young girl comes out on the deck below in a white dress. She seems not to know that I am above. Maybe sixteen years old, in the perfect middle ground between child and woman. I cannot take my eyes from her.

The sun peeks over the edge of the world. I can see her hair taken back by the breeze. She reaches with her hand and pushes the thin strap of her dress free of her shoulder. Her other hand reaches over and does the same. The sheer white dress drops around her ankles in folds on the deck. She steps over the dress and walks to the edge of the stern. Her skin is unbelievable. My feeling for her is complete. She dives into the ocean. And she is gone. My eyes rest again on her empty dress, white on white.

•

Everyone has experienced deja vu. I found a book in here that gives an explanation. The book says it's a brain skip. Our long-term memory steps ahead of the short-term memory. We are actually remembering something as it happens. Our memory is racing alongside reality, maybe trying to replace this world with the world inside our minds.

While I am having these dreams, I can actually remember what's going to happen next. I can tell myself, "This is only a dream," but I can't seem to change the outcome. Whatever the explanation, these dreams are gifts from God. I am allowed to feel the ocean breeze, the spray on my face, the fear, guilt, terror of the book bag, and the warmth from the sight of that girl without ever leaving my bunk.

blood and the tiger

I remember walking with my mother down a street in a small town. At least I think it's a memory. I can't really be sure. We're holding hands. I'm maybe eight or nine years old.

My mother is wearing a blue dress, light blue. The kind women wore back then. Not too short, not too long. A summer dress, white and light blue. Her hair has recently been done. I can tell by the tightness and its refusal to move in the breeze. She has a white purse in her other hand. It hangs by the side of her dress, swinging slightly as she walks, brushing the fabric making a swishing noise as we go. She seems very pretty, and I wonder if other people think she is pretty.

We pass the hardware store, and the beauty shop. My mother's shoes tap each step. My tennis shoes are silent. Our hands are loosely held, my left in her right. It isn't a protective grip, or one that encourages a child's discipline. Instead, it is the comfortable touch of two people, a mother and her boy, walking leisurely down a small town street, with no particular time to be anywhere, for any reason. We are holding hands because we like it.

Above my tennis shoes the cuffs of my blue jeans are rolled. My mother rolled them up. They're too long, but she expects I will grow so she just rolls them up for now. My shirt is checkered, and tucked in, with seven baseball cards in my top pocket. I have memorized the batting averages of all seven players. The numbers have taken their places in my mind like the words of the Pledge of

Allegiance. They will stay there beyond this walk on the town street, or the next morning, or maybe even next summer.

We walk on past the post office. My mother is smiling. Her smile reminds me of the sun in the morning when I wake up and look out my bedroom window. It is hard to turn my face away from my mother's smile. It seems to flow from her face, down her arm, and into my hand. The light blue in her dress seems brightened by her smile. Up ahead I can see the top of a Ferris wheel in the park. The traveling circus arrived yesterday and it covers me up with curiosity and excitement and anticipation. But it will be there when we arrive. There is no need to hurry. Pink cotton candy and row after row of big floppy stuffed animals wait for me. It's me and my mother the whole circus waits for. Who else could it be?

Mr. Gentry waves from the courthouse steps as we pass. My mother waves back. He watches us after she has turned her head. Even at eight years old, some instinct, a God-given instinct, tells me he has a separate reason for watching my mother. Another instinct, also God-given, tells me to squeeze her hand a little tighter. I am a future man.

There are elephants tied up outside. They sway side to side, swatting flies, following us with their tiny eyes on the sides of their huge gray heads. People eat snowcones, and hotdogs, and pay money to play target games. On one side of the big tent are rides and games. On the other side are the animals. Mom has already told me we can't stay for the show. We've got to be home. Today is the day Daddy started his new job.

My mother walks me to the tiger cage. His mouth is open, and he pants for more air. He seems to see me. Seems to look directly at me. The tiger rises from his place in the floor and walks to the metal bars of the cage. At eye level I can see red-caked blood on his big meaty paw as he watches me. I can feel my mother squeeze my hand just slightly as we wait.

I miss my mother very much. I miss her every day.

letters to Janie (4th letter)

Janie,

I sometimes think about our baby. When you told me you were pregnant, I didn't know what to say. I waited and watched your face to decide if I should be happy or sad. Inside I wanted to be happy, even though you cried the way you did.

Remember? We got out the calendar, back-tracked, tried to figure out how and when one crazy sperm struck gold. For some stupid reason I was proud. I couldn't stop smiling. We were unemployed, drunk half the time, nowhere to go, but I couldn't stop smiling. Somehow, someway, in this big nasty world, God, or nature, or some force, cared about one thing, survival. Full dog eat dog, burn the bridges, a flower blooms in a nuclear junkyard, survival of me, and you, and the whole goddamned species depends on this spear-headed sperm and this little jelly egg bouncing up against each other on a hot pink uterine wall.

We never could pinpoint the day of conception, but I'll always remember the day the baby died. August 31st. It was a Thursday. You said it never was a baby. You said it was a nothing. But it was the realest thing I've ever known.

If God is all-knowing, and all-powerful, He would certainly be capable of creating other beings like himself; all-knowing, all-perfect. Instead, He created us. And knowing we were not perfect, or anywhere close, He created a world of temptations. Temptations of the flesh, money, power, greed, and wickedness. And then He dropped us, imperfect, weak, afraid, into this world of trouble.

Why would He do this to us? Shit, why would He do this to Himself? Imagine the world He could have created, full of little Gods, not just in the image of the big God, but identical. A world in which we'd choose against the Devil every day, not because we have to, but because we know better. Little Gods would never choose a three-second orgasm with a back-room whore over a lifetime of loyalty with the mother of their children.

"And I give them eternal life, and they shall never perish. No one can take them out of my hand. My Father who has given them to me, is greater than all and no one can take them out of the Father's hand. The Father and I are one." John 10:28-30.

•

I want a grave to visit. But there's nothing. Just your word that our baby died before it had a chance to live. You wouldn't let me give it a name. You wouldn't let me bury it. One day I had my hand on your belly, talking softly through your skin to my little boy, and the next day we were smoking cigarettes and fuckin' on the floor again, all wadded up like a chalk ball in the throat of this pitiful illusion. When that baby died, it actually brought me to my knees.

Gabriel Black

Greta Braun
(letter from a juror received six months
after I was sentenced to prison)

Dear Mr. Black,

I served on your jury last April. I have done a great deal of thinking since we were in court. I am a Christian, and as a Christian, I believe that you are a child of God, however misguided or lost.

You should know that we jurors did not take our responsibility lightly. Several of us believe the woman was far more involved than she admitted. Several others wanted only to convict you of the lesser charge of manslaughter. At the end of the first day we voted 6 for manslaughter and 6 for murder. On the morning of the second day I asked whether everyone in the room believed in God. The answer from all was "yes." On my suggestion, we held hands and prayed silently for the insight and strength to make the right decision. Twelve strangers sat together hand in hand around a table for over 5 minutes of complete and total quiet. It was spiritual, Mr. Black. Afterwards, we wrote our votes on pieces of paper and handed them to the foreman. All 12 jurors voted for the murder charge.

I believe that the 12 people in the jury room were guided by the Lord. Now, as a Christian, I extend my hand to you so that you may learn from your sins and find Jesus. If Jesus had been with you on that fateful day, I dare say you would not be behind bars. If you had chosen the Lord and His glory over the tingle in your loins,

I dare say you would not have found yourself standing over the bloody body of your lover's husband.

Now you must take responsibility for your deeds. You must confess your sins and ask the Lord for forgiveness. You must be saved and rid yourself of the false idea that a man can save himself. For not only can a man not save himself, but the longer he clings to the idea of being his own savior, the more hopelessly desperate he becomes. As we all know, desperation leads away from salvation.

If you write to me, I will write back.

Together in Christ,

Greta Braun

•

I never wrote her back. I read the letter out loud one day to John and Crazy Carl Anderson. Carl listened closely and squinted his little eyes at the end. The space between Carl Anderson and Greta Braun is so deep, and so wide, I do not believe all the words in the world could fill the gap. It is hard to believe they could exist at the same time, on the same planet. They know nothing about each other, and never will.

conscience

When I was a kid in school, sixth grade, I found fifteen dollars in a yellow envelope in a trash can near the playground. The envelope had a teacher's name written on the outside and some papers inside with three five-dollar bills. We divided the money. Me and Mike Sewell and a kid named Gilbert. Each of us took five dollars, and I threw the envelope back in the trash with the papers.

All the way home on the bus I imagined ways to get the five-dollar bill into my home. I came up with a dozen schemes and stories to explain where the money came from. My brother met me at the bus stop on his bicycle. As we headed home, it hit me. I waited for him to turn his head, and then I dropped the five-dollar bill on the ground by the side of the road.

"Look! Look what I found. It's a five-dollar bill. It was right here by the road. A five-dollar bill."

My brother was amazed. He spent fifteen minutes searching around in the grass for another five-dollar bill. When we got home he went to my mother, as I knew he would, and told the story. I showed everybody the money and went to my room.

Later that night the phone rang. The teacher had heard about us finding the money which was accidentally thrown away. She called our parents and asked us to bring it back the next day. I could overhear the phone conversation from my room. I listened to my mother's footsteps as she made the long walk down the short hall.

I've thought about this story a million times. Why did I feel the need to fake finding the money on the side of the road? Why couldn't I have just walked into the house with the five-dollar bill folded neatly in the back pocket of my blue jeans? Why couldn't I have gone to the store after school like the other two guys and bought five dollars worth of candy and baseball cards?

Why? Because God gave me a conscience. A conscience so strong that it never crossed my mind to just walk through my front door with a five-dollar bill in my pocket that didn't belong to me. A conscience so strong that it screamed to get caught or somehow make it right. Just a thin piece of paper, wrinkled and green, but it weighed a ton in my mind. Why would God give me such a conscience, and then when I use this conscience to step forward for Janie, to take responsibility, He punishes me with a lifetime in this place?

The world looks different from the bottom of a barrel. And, trust me, it is different. Take away everything you depend on. Take away your money, and everything your money buys for you. Take away your mother and father, your wife or husband. Take away your children you say you live for. Take away your safety nets, all the locked doors, all your policies, retirement accounts. Take away your football heroes. And time. The infrastructure of your day and night. The measurement of everything you do, you plan to do, you already did. Lay it down, look at it, and take it away.

Now try to see yourself. There's nowhere you need to be, and no one who cares. You wake up, eat, shit, sleep, wake up, eat, and shit again. There are no Mondays, or Saturdays, because what's the difference? There's no day next week or particular night next month that you look forward to, which helps you get past the bad days. No such thing. And there's no hope of any such thing.

There is a blackness. A dark, lonely place deep in the middle of a moonless night. In a corner, unable to see even the outline of your own hand six inches from your face. A blackness with no measure, dimension, or blue-black motion. It is a place where a man, if left too long, can lose himself. It is a place where the difference between living and dying is the difference between black and black.

Sometimes it seems I have come full circle. I wonder if these doubts in God are for a reason. They say that God never puts more on you than you can carry. When He does, when He goes too far, how will I know? When He breaks his own rule, what happens next?

books

When I came here, I probably hadn't read two books in my entire life. They didn't exist for me. My mother and my father never talked about books. We didn't have any in our house. If I had never come to prison, I would've never known the magic and the power. They have changed me. Not just on the surface, with new words and ideas, but inside of me, I am better.

The only true test of whether I like a book is if I keep reading it. There's no one to impress in here. There's no reason to walk around with a fancy title under my arm. I have put down fat books after only a few pages and felt no urge to ever pick them up again. So I never did. When a book is really good, there doesn't need to be an explanation. After a dozen pages I can feel the sadness of coming to its last page.

Graham Greene, *The Heart of the Matter*. If you're Catholic, and I am, put it under your pillow. It can crawl around in the empty space under your beliefs like an old dog, a steady moaning under the floorboard.

All the King's Men, Robert Penn Warren. By the time I finished his book I emptied two ink pens underlining parts to go back and read. Jesus, how does a man write such a thing? A writer's certain words, certain phrases, strung together like beads on a string, can leave me feeling outside of myself, outside the walls of this prison. Books have become my sanctuary. Books are my way to worship alone in a church full of atheists, and liars, and gigantic motherfuckers who want to shove things inside me.

They can scream all night, spit through the bars, sling handfuls of shit across the hall, but after the second page, maybe the third, "nothing beside remains, round that colossal wreck, boundless and bare, the lone and level sands stretch far away" (Percy Shelley).

God gave me these books. God gave me these books, and He gave the people who wrote them some alien ability to communicate worlds in words. There is no other explanation I can find.

Cormac McCarthy, *Blood Meridian*. An attack, not just an attack, a seizure. A seizure on your gut belief that life is important. After I finished the book it took me three days to figure out I wasn't sick. I went to the prison doctor twice. I put the book away several times and picked it up again.

•

It is the recognition and the creation of a different reality. Crazy Carl Anderson does it for himself. Writers do it for me. I wonder if some people have an extra part of their brain, a survival mechanism which turns on and off allowing them to create in their minds, or on paper, a separate reality, the discovery of a thin difference. It's borderline insanity.

Albert Einstein wrote, "Great spirits have always encountered violent resistance from mediocre minds."

It's an interesting use of the words. He says, "great spirits". He doesn't say, "great men," or "great people." He says, "always," not just "sometimes." He says, "violent resistance," not just "resistance," or "defiance," or "behind the scenes sabotage". It's "violent". And then he says, "mediocre minds." He doesn't say, "fools," or "idiots."

The mediocre minds always resist violently. They have to. They have no other choice. The walls they have built around themselves are sacred. They were built to keep people out, not to keep people in. The same book which allows me to fly outside these concrete prison walls, threatens another man who has spent his life building his own imaginary concrete walls.

The *Fountainhead* by Ayn Rand. It is the only book in this world I have read more than once. I will read it every few years until I die. It is the spiritual equivalent to diving headfirst on a hot summer day into the waters of a cool, clear lake. The only bad part is coming back up again.

choices

I had this dream. I call it a dream because I don't know what else to call it.

I walked in and sat down at a table in a small white room. There was one chair on the other side of the table. A man came in the opposite door and walked easily to the empty chair. He sat down. I remember everything about him, as if I had seen him before, wearing the same clothes, with the same expression on his face. There was no one else in the room, and the room was empty except for the table and chairs and us.

"Gabriel?"

"Yes."

"Do you know who I am?"

"I'm not sure."

"Gabriel, I look different to different people. I look, and act, and speak the way each person imagines, somewhere in the backs of their minds, how I should look, act, and speak. I am God. Some see me old and some see me young. Some see me as a woman. Others imagine me dressed in flowing white clothes. I am seen as a buffalo, the sun, or a volcano. It doesn't matter. I am God."

He was wearing a flannel shirt, neatly pressed and buttoned at the cuffs. There was nothing at all distinctive about this middle-aged man. He was a man you could pass on the street and never think about again.

"I am the one who created all that you know. I set in motion your life, and the lives around you. Sometimes, not often, but sometimes, I step in and make a few adjustments. This is one of those times.

"I have a proposition for you, Gabriel. Listen carefully. You are just a young man of eighteen, and today you have a choice to make.

"In each life there is hardship. It is the way I made the world, and it is the way it will stay. Some carry a heavier burden than others, and more often than you know it is I who make those decisions. Some of you believe that you are, each of you, where you exist according to decisions you have made yourself. That is only partly right. Today, you will make one of those decisions, and set a course never to be altered.

"Between yourself, your mother, your brother, and your best friend, one of you will spend most of your life in prison, and one of you will lose a baby. Two heavy burdens.

"If you will agree to carry both of these burdens, I will spare your mother, your brother, and your best friend from these hardships. If you will agree now to lose a baby in your lifetime, and go to prison at some point, for most of your life, we will shake hands, and you, Gabriel Black, will have made a decision like the decisions I make every second, of every day, of eternity."

I listened to each word. As I would think of a question, the answer would follow inside my mind. There was no need to speak my questions. The man's hands were folded together on the table between us. His expression was blank, and then I remembered that his expression was whatever I wished it to be.

I reached my right hand across the table and held it open. The man lifted his right hand and placed it in mine. We shook three times and separated.

"The deal is done, Gabriel Black. There will be no

reward for making this choice other than the knowledge that you were faced with this decision and made the choice that you made."

The man rose slowly, turned his back, and walked through the door. It closed behind him, and I was left alone in a little white room sitting at the table.

predestination

Cannibals don't eat clowns. The world has no reason to destroy the idiot. They are the clowns of God, protected. The world saves its vengeance for the man who tries to succeed, at anything, for any purpose. We stand together, all of us in a huddled mass, hating the man who separates himself from the crowd through his genius, or ability, or clean competence. We embrace the shove forward by these men into the future, but their very existence is a reminder of our weakness. It is the combination of this prayer and savage resistance which separates us into categories of apparent happiness.

Would I have been better off wallowing on the warm couch, ignoring the man as he busted through the door? Maybe. I could have ignored the fear, or maybe felt no fear at all. But those are two different things. And after all, I never really had those choices. It was my destiny at that moment to step up and take the world's tight fist against my chest, in a worse way than the bullet that left its hole in the skin of a dead man. I was wound up and set in motion by a God with thin fingers, with a purpose, with a knowledge that I would stumble around for the years of my life like a toy soldier bumping into walls until that certain day. And then on that certain day I had no more choice than the toy soldier, winding down, weakly kicking the wall, knowing it will never move.

If I am to believe in predestination, then I must believe it all makes some slow-moving dark-colored sense. I need to see it soon.

hope

People seem to naturally turn towards God when they have lost control of their lives. There is no place in the world like prison to make a person feel he has lost control of his life. I have watched men sit in their cells and read the Bible all day long. Men who never thought twice in the outside world about the Bible or Jesus or the stories told in the book. I have tried hard not to make my decisions about God from a position of fear, or loneliness, or a total loss of control. It is not easy when I am told every day like a child where I will sleep, when I will eat, or when I will clean myself. My mail is opened, my room is searched. Other people decide my choices of magazines, books, television shows, clothes, underwear, toilet paper, toothpaste, sheets, pillows, food, and even friends.

But hope can live in the tiniest corners. I spent almost two years planning to escape. John and I discussed it every day between ourselves. We kept notes about the schedules of guards, and jotted diagrams of the buildings and fences. We would think up plans and then eliminate ideas one by one, keeping certain parts of each plan which seemed useful. We had little hiding places for our notes and diagrams.

John was very good at the ideas. We would always get around to talking about what would happen when we were free. Where we would go, how we would establish new identities, and how we would go see all the things we always wanted to see. I would read in newspapers about men who escaped from prison and got caught in only a few days or a few weeks. They would mostly say things like, "I got drunk every day and slept in the back of an old pickup truck."

John and I would agree how stupid those guys must be. To have a chance at freedom, minute-by-minute freedom, to choose for yourself where to go and when to get there, and then choose to stay drunk and sleep in the back of a pickup truck until some cop drives by and takes your ass back to prison.

We knew if we could just resist the urges to get drunk and chase whores and go see our old friends, we could stay free forever. But I guess that's probably not what it's like. How do you feel free when you're looking over your shoulder every minute? How do you feel like you're making your own choices when every choice is based on not getting caught, not being recognized? How do you get money to live? And where do you live in a world that refuses to recognize your freedom?

After you're in here long enough, you forget how to live. The world passes you by. There's nobody out there who knows me anymore. I can't work the computers I read about. John says they cripple us on purpose, the way they tie up a horse's leg to keep him from walking away. The way they made it illegal to teach a slave to read so he couldn't learn about his predicament.

I know now that we would never have really tried to escape. The little diagrams ended up in the toilet and our crazy plans ended up seeming stupid. But it wasn't about escaping physically. It was about hope. It was about lying awake at night after all the whispering and planning, and imagining waking up in a real bed, with a real woman, and eating breakfast. It was about deciding for yourself all those little decisions that separate us from the animals.

There were times it seemed so real I could almost taste a hotdog at the baseball game. I could see the face of my son watching the foul ball in the blue sky get closer and closer to our seats down the third-base line. The ball would land with a pop in his leather glove and my wife, my beautiful wife, would smile at us as I took the ball from his glove and held it up to my face. There is nothing like the smell of a baseball. Nothing.

the ancient art of masturbation

punchin' the clown
spankin' the monkey
rollin' the raddish
whackin', jackin',
smackin' the midget

Catholics believe that the sexual act exists for the sole purpose of making a baby. We believe it is wrong for a man to wear a rubber because the rubber gets in the way. I never could understand why it was acceptable for a Catholic couple to use modern knowledge and technology to figure out what days are safe to have sex without making a baby, but then they couldn't use a thin piece of rubber to accomplish the same goal. The rules never made much sense to me.

Carl Anderson masturbates at least three times a day. He doesn't ask himself any questions, he just does it, the same way he eats when he's hungry and sleeps when he's tired. His mental illness, whatever the hell it is, complicates everything. Last week he stabbed himself in the scrotum with a fork. He stretched out the loose skin and stabbed through it with the four points of the fork stolen from the guard's mess. Carl hadn't thought about it enough to figure out he'd end up with eight holes in his scrotum instead of only four. He hadn't thought about it, and he really didn't care. Something inside Carl decided masturbation just wasn't enough on that particular day.

Leon asked, "Hey, Carl, why you been up at the infirmary?"

"None of your business, asshole."

"How'd they close them holes up so you don't leak out?"

"I don't know what you talkin' about, Leon. You need to spend more time worryin' about your own damn self."

Leon smiled and reached into his pocket. He pulled out a fork and held it up. Leon pointed with the index finger of the other hand and counted slowly.

"One. Two. Three. Four. Four points on a fork, Carl."

Carl stood up from his bunk and tried to chase Leon Evers out of the room, but he stopped in the middle of his first step and grabbed his sore balls.

•

When I was fourteen years old my mother sent me off to a Catholic retreat for altar boys. There were three of us from the local parish who went to the big city. I'd never seen girls like that before. They came up to the altar, one by one, taking communion. It was a constant struggle to resist the movement of my imagination towards lust.

I pretended I was sick one Sunday and a girl named Lila Chandler snuck back to my room. I could hear the booming voice of the priest during Mass as I struggled to unlock her bra. It was like cracking the safe at Fort Knox. I kept hearing footsteps outside the door. She'd giggle like I was an idiot. The priest's voice seemed louder and louder. And then I lost my load. It happened in an instant. It felt like a robust explosion in my pants. While it was actually happening, while I was in the middle of that concentration of satisfaction, I can remember wondering if Lila Chandler knew what was happening. And then I let out this grunt. It came from down inside my teenage chest. A grunt. She stood up, bra strap still in place, and looked down at me like I was a puppy who just shit on the carpet.

If I'd killed Lila Chandler, right then, right there, my life would have been different. Instead, she told everyone in the world who would sit still long enough to listen. She told the boys from my hometown, and she told the girls. I stood in that big beautiful church three more Sundays. I would stare down at my feet during Mass, afraid to look up into the eyes of anyone.

On the last day Father Shannon asked, "Gabriel, is there anything you need to confess, anything you need to talk about?"

Did he know?

"No, Father, there's nothing."

As I rode home on the bus I remember wondering which sin would land me in hell. Lying to a Priest, or those few seconds of unbearable pleasure my body gave me as a punishment for wanting to see Lila Chandler's boobs.

•

There is only one physical feeling I have ever had which compares to the orgasm. Poison ivy. If you take your hands, covered with the bumps and blisters of poison ivy, and hold them under running hot water, you will feel what I mean. It is concentrated satisfaction. It is a thousand scratches in a few seconds' time. When we are hungry, it takes minutes to satisfy the hunger. When we are tired, it takes hours to satisfy the body. When we have an orgasm, our sexual urges are satisfied in only a few seconds.

Years after the fork problem, Carl Anderson found a tiny poison ivy vine in the recreation yard. He would take a leaf and rub it on his hands, squeezing out all the juice in the tiny leaf. When his hands were puffed and red, oozing with that amber liquid, Carl would go to the big sink in the back of the kitchen, turn the water as hot as it would go, and hold his hands under as long as he could. His eyes would roll back in his head and he would ring his hands together like a madman. Unfortunately, Carl went back to masturbating and poison ivy spread all through the crooks and cracks of Carl Anderson like rot weed.

●

I'm not sure what all this means. There are just so few real pleasures. I am a man who is denied the right to touch a woman, and I have been denied this right for so many years. Yet my hand can reach my dick, and my urges are there every hour of every hopeless day, and my imagination is strong, and God gave me my hand, and my dick, and my urges, and my imagination. And He made my private orgasm, with no hope of procreation, just as intense, just as satisfying, as that man in a condominium at the beach on top of his pretty little wife in the middle of her cycle.

I don't need to understand it.

Dear Janie,

If your husband had not come over that morning and you had not shot him dead, I believe you would have been easy to forget. The next woman would have made you forgettable. Unfortunately, there was no next woman, and I am stuck with your memory forever.

It has been a long time since I wrote you a letter. I promised myself this time to write the letter and send it on the same day instead of reading and rereading the damn thing over and over for weeks, imagining you reading it.

I halfway expected to see you at my hearing for a new trial. Instead, I had to sit in the courtroom with your husband's mother and sisters and listen to them spew their crap. My desire to convince them of the truth went away a long time ago. I knew I had no chance when that woman stood up from her wheelchair with a picture of her dead son. If I had been the judge, I wouldn't have given me a new trial either. Besides, we all knew it was a waste of time.

During the woman's long rambling speech, she never mentioned you once. Your name never came up. I thought that was amazing. You killed the man, the son of the lady in the wheelchair, the man in that picture she kept waving around, and nobody ever mentioned your name at all. Just like you never existed. Just like I killed a stranger on the street, at random, because I hated the way he looked, or he cut me off in traffic.

When I sat there silent in that chair, there was some lonely calm in knowing that I was the only person in the room who knew what happened. I stopped listening to those people and wondered about facing God when I die. I wondered who will be in the room when God decides if I will go to Heaven. Will He explain to that lady in the wheelchair what really happened? I think so. Will you be in the room? I think so. Not for revenge. Just to put an end to it. Just to finally put it to rest. Or maybe just so I can rest.

I don't think about where you are anymore. I don't think about whether you are married or have children or if you think about me. Mostly I try to put you, and the memory of you, in some proper place in my life. I try to figure out how it all fits in the universe with God's big plan. I know now that I did this to myself. I made decisions that put me in the middle of a situation where I had no business. I put myself in the hands of people who had no business with my life in their hands. And now my freedom is in the fists of politicians, and prison guards, and people who have never met me. But my life, who I really am, will always be in God's hands, and no one, not you or anyone else, can change that.

Gabriel

fire

They say that every fire is part of every other fire.

Eddie Mueller, the boy who ate the crow head, came to my cell one day. Somehow he got his hands on a pack of matches. I can't figure him out. There are days he sits and stares at the wall, and there are other days he gets focused on some fucked-up, off-the-wall idea. This was one of those days.

"Mr. Black, I need to speak with you."

Eddie's matted hair swung with his head as he looked back and forth at me and out the door. His hands were raw and red.

"How do you build a fire?"

He sat down on the far end of the bed. His fingers fiddled with a little blue book of matches.

"What kind of fire, Eddie?"

He hesitated, "Just a fire. Like a fire in the fireplace. What goes on top of what?"

"Well, I guess you can put some paper on the bottom. My father used to roll newspaper longways and tie it in knots. Maybe put some dry sticks on top of the paper. Give it something to catch. Then on top of the sticks you'd put your bigger logs."

Eddie listened closely. His hands fidgeted. His eyes looked at my mouth like he could see the words come out.

"What else?"

"Well, you need to make sure it's all dry. You need to give it plenty of air. Then just light it and let it go."

Eddie's eyes changed on the word "air."

"Why? Why's it need air?"

"Fire needs oxygen. It needs oxygen as much as it needs something to burn."

Eddie Mueller said, "Fire breathes like us, don't it? It eats and it breathes, just like us. It finally dies out, like we do, but then it comes back, somewhere else. You can't ever put out all the fires in the world."

I just watched him. He sat for a while and didn't say anything, suddenly calm and quiet. He held out his hand with the little pack of matches in the palm.

He said, "I got some matches." And then he left the room.

A few days later the fire alarms went off in the middle of the night. I could see a yellow glow at the other end of the hall.

Eddie Mueller had built a fire. He took old newspapers he'd hidden away and rolled them longways. He placed them under his bed and put books from the library on top of the newspapers. He put socks and shirts and anything that would burn around the pile. Then Eddie Mueller must have pulled out his little pack of blue matches and lit the paper. He crawled into his bed and pulled the covers up to his chin. The fire burned his body into a crispy mess like a dead Viking on a funeral pyre. The man never made a sound. It stunk like rotten burnt meat for a week.

I've wondered what frame of mind he was in. Was he in his crazy mind and didn't know what he was doing, or was he in his right mind and just tired of living? But there never was really a question. No one in his right mind would burn himself to death. Would he?

•

John told me a story about how his mother died. On his parents' twentieth anniversary she spent the day getting the house ready for her husband to come home from work. She made arrangements for John and his sister to stay with relatives after school. John's mother cleaned the house and cooked the perfect dinner. She put candles around the house and on the dining room table. She put on a white kimono her husband had given her the Christmas before.

John's father was supposed to be home at 6:30, but he was running late. When he pulled up in the driveway his house was a giant inferno. He could see the fire churning the ceiling and leaping out the windows upstairs. The firemen were running left and right with great spirals of water shooting into the air. I have tried to remember some of John's words when he told the story.

They believe his mother was lighting the candles on the table. The sleeve from the white kimono caught fire and she fell to the floor. The fire jumped to the rug, and maybe then the tablecloth, and John's mother burned like Eddie Mueller in a spit of flame and fire and red hot wind.

Only God could make fire. It doesn't fit with anything else. It eats and breathes. It destroys and kills with beautiful colors and graceful fluid motions. No wonder a common characteristic of the mentally ill is their fascination with fire. No man or woman of this earth could create such a thing.

letter from father

Gabriel,

Its been to long since we talked. I went to your mommas grave yesterday in the old cemetery. She'd a rolled over if she'd known I was there. I was just glad she couldn't see me. I don't look to good no more. I'm not sure I ever looked to good.

Your brother got his life straight. He don't call me, but I seen him one day at the grocery store last year before I moved. His little boy didn't even know me. When you was little you used to look at me like I was a stranger. Are you ever getting out of that place. Sometimes I don't remember to good. Maybe they wont ever let you out. Maybe you should stay there till you die for what you done to those people. Johnny's little boy wouldn't shake my hand. He was scared of his own grandfather. He don't even known me, and he was scared. He hid behind his daddy like a little dog. Johnny gave me $20 out of his pocket.

That old bitch trys to make me take my medicine. Sometimes I take it, sometimes I don't. Medicine don't work on me. Never has. Do you remember the time you killed your dog with that arrow. I come home from work and that dog was dead in the front yard. I had to bury it. I always had to do the burying. I was the one who had to clean up the mess. I dug a hole in the backyard and dropped that dog in the bottom. The arrow was still sticking out his belly. Two days later that hole got dug up by some animal. The dog was pulled up and eaten in two pieces. I never told you that because you was just a boy and I didn't see no reason to tell you that. What the Hell was that dogs name. I dont reckon you'll ever know the difference between right and wrong. You was always a liar. You was always sneaking around hiding in your momma's arms. There ain't nothing easy about this life boy. It dont get easier when you get old. I'm just waiting to die. Thats all Im doing. Im just waiting to die. Your mothers gone. Your in prison. Your brother dont call me, and my grandson dont know me. It ain't nobodys fault but my own. I was to busy. Busy with shit that dont matter. You got to get right with God. I was never right with the old man. Once you get on his bad side, its hard as Hell to get back on the good side. That old man makes you pay for your mistakes one way or the other. He'll give you to much or give you nothing and let you learn your lessons the hard way.

I don't even have the pleasure of guilt. I ain't got no grounds to make you or anybody else feel guilty about me. Your momma could make me feel guilty in a New York split second with the roll of those black shark eyes or a shake of her head. But she had grounds. I ain't got no grounds. When your young its hard to see the future. It didn't cross my mind that all them stupid decisions would come back one by one to haunt me like the devil. I just kept making stupid decisions. I just kept making promises I couldn't keep. Like coaching your little league football team. It seems like every year you'd ask and I'd promise, and every year I'd have a new excuse. New job. To busy. Never could make the time. Not that it would've made a God damned difference. What makes a man piss his life away. What kind of God given instinct makes a man pick whiskey over his wife, and lying over his boys, and sleeping late over going to work and getting an education. I scratched my balls while the house burned down.

Don't count on me to write again. Hell, I may be dead before I can stick a stamp on this envelope and they might be given this letter to you at my funeral. Will they let you come to your pappas funeral. Make sure those son of a bitches bury me in that big green cemetry next to your momma. Nobody ever loved me like she did. Nobody ever held me like your momma. I hope she made some friends in heaven. I'm gonna need the votes.

Pop Eye

•

The handwriting tilts upwards from left to right and there are coffee stains across the bottom. The envelope had no return address and a postmark from somewhere in Kentucky. I never heard from my father again. I don't know if he is alive or dead. There isn't much difference.

a brilliant blue day

I never paid much attention to a beautiful day when I was free. A beautiful day takes on a new meaning in prison. It's kind of like having the flu. When you're throwing up with your head in the toilet, not able to eat or think straight, all you want is to feel normal again. When you're feeling that way, all you can imagine is how great it will be when you're finally not sick. Then you start to feel better, and it only takes a few hours before you begin taking for granted feeling good. You'll have to wait until you're sick again to appreciate the feeling.

It's the same way with a beautiful day. When I was a kid, growing up where I grew up, we played football down at Lambert's field almost every afternoon. The sky would be a bright blue and sometimes we'd actually pray for rain so we could make spectacular tackles in the mud. We'd say Hail Mary's while the Methodist boys would stare at us like we were people from the jungles of South America.

Even though I had a limp I was quick. I learned early that I could overcome my limp by playing smart. We'd play until dark or until somebody's mother called them home and messed up the teams in the middle of a game. When a kid would get hurt, we stood around half-concerned and half-afraid. Cary Hanson caught a pass next to the Lambert's house and slid on his knees. A big jagged rock cut up his knee. He didn't cry. He just looked at it like it was someone else's knee. One by one we all told Cary that it was nothing, just a little cut, put a Band-Aid on it, it'll be all right. His mother took him to the hospital and he got eleven stitches. The scar was a badge of honor.

Every year my Catholic School would have a big fair. There were rides, and games, and beer for the grown-ups. Father Jacoby would get red-eyed and take over the mouse game. He would spin a big wheel which stood like a table four or five feet above the ground. There were different colored holes the size of fifty-cent pieces around the outside of the wheel. People would place their bets on the color of their choice, and Father Jacoby would let a white mouse loose on the spinning table. We would yell and scream at that mouse until he crawled down a hole. If he crawled down the hole you bet on, you'd win. The maximum bet was a quarter.

One year me and Cary Hanson stole the white mouse and replaced it with a rat we caught in the woods behind Lambert's field. The rat was big and brown and pissed off. As usual, Father Jacoby drank more beers than we could count. He called everyone to the mouse table and didn't bother to check the little cage underneath. He talked up the game and encouraged everyone to place their bets.

"It's for a good cause, son. Pick your favorite color. Any color you want. Ma'am, you can double that quarter in just a few seconds."

The wheel spun with a flick of Father Jacoby's wrist and in a quick motion the man snatched up the little cage and dumped that big damned swamp rat on the spinning board of holes and colors. There was no way that big son-of-a-bitch could fit down one of those holes. He ran smack into the little clear plastic wall separating the spectators from the wheel. Before anyone knew what had happened, that damned rat hopped like a rabbit over the little wall and landed in a baby stroller with Tommy Kane's baby sister.

Women were screaming and people were knocking each other down to get away. The dizzy, scared, brown rat wedged himself under the baby and Tommy Kane's mother fainted like a wet rag and fell on the ground. I guess the thought of a rat in a stroller cuddled up next to her baby is more than a mother can possibly endure.

The closest man to the stroller reached his hand in to try to pull out that damned rat and got bit. His eyes got wide and he yanked his hand out with that rat's teeth buried in the web-skin between his thumb and index finger. I believe that rat had given up on any chance of living and decided he'd die with style.

There wasn't any time to laugh yet. Father Jacoby spilled his beer, and the man with the rat on his hand started screaming like he had fire up his ass. The harder he'd swing his hand around, the deeper that rat's teeth would clinch. He beat it on the big wheel and punched it with his free hand. The rat wouldn't let loose. The whole damned fair nearly shut down. The people on top of the Ferris wheel were pointing. Two policemen ran over ready to break up a fight only to find a man with a rat on his hand.

The next year at the fair the mouse table was gone. Father Jacoby launched a full-scale investigation but never could figure out who switched the rodents. He called me into his office.

"Gabriel, you know why you're here?"

"No, Father."

"I saw you at the fair near the table where Mr. Woodward was bitten."

"I was there. Is Mr. Woodward O.K.?"

Father Jacoby smiled. I knew it was some sort of trick.

"Gabriel, do you think it was funny?"

I didn't answer.

He smiled again and said, "It was a funny idea. There's no way a person could know it would end up the way it did."

I remember turning my eyes from Father Jacoby and looking out his window. It was a beautiful blue day. Not a single cloud in the sky. I knew as soon as we got home from school we'd be down at Lambert's lot with a football. I knew we'd be laughing about Mr. Woodward, and Tommy Kane's mother fainting, and that rat flying through the air like it was shot from a cannon, landing in that baby carriage. I remember out of the corner of my eye seeing Father Jacoby turn his head and look with me out the window at the blue sky. It seems like we sat that way for a long time.

consequences

A new kid showed up last week. Young. Named Mark. He's twenty-five years old, and looks about fuckin' fifteen.

I said, "What the hell are you in here for?"

"Statutory rape."

"Statutory rape?"

"Yes, sir."

"Don't call me sir. Save it for the guards and the guys you'll meet in the shower."

"What guys?"

I could tell he wasn't stupid. He would learn a lot in the next six months about the rotten underbelly of this life. His eyes were wide open, but with a strange indifference.

"How old was she?"

"Fourteen."

"How many years did you get?"

"Ten split with two to serve. Her mother wanted me dead."

I laughed and said, "I hope it was worth it."

He smiled and turned away like a kid who already knows. Mark said, "It was."

"You're telling me that one night with this fourteen-year-old girl is worth two years of your life in the penitentiary eatin' dog food and sleepin' with one eye open and one hand over your balls?"

"Yes, sir."

"You won't be sayin' that shit in a few weeks."

"I think I will."

"Why?"

Not only was he not stupid, I started to see that he was smart. Behind the smile, there was a glaze of calm across his face, which in a place like this is rare even for old bastards like me.

"Mr. Black, I wouldn't change any of it."

"Knowing you'd end up here, knowing she was only fourteen, you'd do it all over again?"

Mark hesitated, not over his answer, but over the memory.

"Yes, sir, I would do it again," he paused. "I'd rather be in prison, for the rest of my life, and have the memory of that hour, than to be free and live without the memory."

It was genuine. Some people in this place crawl inside themselves and play the tough guy to survive. Mark Rolland genuinely made a choice, suffered the consequences, and was prepared to live with whatever happened next, surrounded by the warm waters of one hour with some idea of an angel with perfect skin.

"Do you think it's going to be enough, boy?"

"What do you mean?"

"Do you think the memory is going to be strong enough to get you through this, and then get you through life as an ex-convict, labeled a sexual predator? Do you think it will be enough when you can't find a job to feed your kids, or own a gun to protect your family, or get permission from your parole officer to move away for a new start, a new start which you can't have anyway because the world believes you're a pervert? You don't know what the fuck you're saying. You don't know what it means to try day after day, year after year, to reconcile your sins and the punishments and the goddamned sickness which comes with running out of time.

"You can say it if you want, Mark, but try not to ignore that your little peace of mind with your one hour of glory is God's way of getting you through this. And He can take it away as fast as He gave it."

Mark watched me closely. He didn't try to understand why I got so angry. His face never showed doubt. We were quiet for a moment. I hoped he would leave. He stood up almost at that exact second and walked to the door of my cell. Before he left the kid stood in the doorway and said, "Mr. Black, you weren't there."

I said back, "No, Mark, I wasn't."

We either survive or we don't. If we do survive, God is the only one who can give us the strength, or wisdom, or weapons we need. If we don't survive, God is the only one who can take away the strength, or wisdom, or weapons and leave us standing alone without guidance to go another minute.

a good story

I was walking back from the yard one day. A folded piece of paper on the ground next to the fence caught my attention. I picked it up and slipped it in my pocket. Outside, on a city street, it's not something a man would pick up, or even notice. But here, I put it in my pocket and took it back to the cell.

It was a story. Written on three pages, small handwriting, folded up neatly, unsigned, and not dated.

CARRY THE BURDEN

She was only four years old. A beautiful little girl with long curly blonde hair and the face of an angel. Her mother went to answer the knock at the door. It was only for a few minutes. There was not enough time to imagine that the little girl could open the back door, walk over to the edge of the pool, slip in, and drown. Her mother found her face down in the shallow end. The minutes stacked on top of each other waiting for the ambulance to arrive. The face of the angel became cold and still.

The funeral man prepared the body. She wore her pink Sunday dress, white shoes, with a ribbon in her hair. Her mother and father stood in the room alone the early morning before the Saturday afternoon funeral. There are no words which exist in this life to console the grief of a mother and father preparing to bury their baby girl. They stood before the coffin on its table, holding hands, crying, wanting to lift her little body into their arms and take her home where she belongs. Death held the door.

She lay peaceful, like a child asleep in her Sunday clothes, waiting for her mother to get ready. Waiting for her father to finish reading the paper.

The funeral director stepped into the room.

The mother asked, "Mr. Baron, will anyone be with her until the funeral this afternoon?"

Mr. Baron was accustomed to such misery in others.

"Mrs. Brooks, we'll be in and out, but no one will actually be sitting with her. You can stay, of course, if you wish."

Mrs. Brooks turned to her husband, with tears in her eyes, and said, "Your father needs us at the house, but she can't be alone. She can't stay here alone. You know how she is. You know she gets afraid."

As the words were spoken, both the mother and father knew that neither could sit next to their little girl in her coffin for those hours. There was simply too much sadness.

"Mr. Baron," she said, "I can't leave her here alone, and it wouldn't be right to leave her with a stranger. Will you allow us to have someone stay here, so she won't be alone? I can't leave her like this."

"Of course, Mrs. Brooks. Of course."

Without speaking, the mother and father of the child began a silent search for the right person in the family. It was probably easy. Me. The child's uncle, the brother of Anna Brooks. I'm sure no one else even entered their minds. They saw me as loyal, and gentle, and the little girl's favorite uncle.

I answered the phone to hear Anna crying. I closed my eyes and listened. There was a pause after the question. I was quick to fill the space with my answer. How could I not? I hung up the phone and stood for a moment contemplating the day. In a crisis, I was always there. Somewhere, long ago, when I was just a boy, it was decided that I would carry the burden. I would set myself aside when necessary and lift the load others could not bear.

I climbed into my expensive car and drove to the funeral home across town. I rolled down the windows on this warm summer morning and purposefully turned off the radio. When I arrived Mr. Baron met me at the door. We exchanged a glance, and Mr. Baron walked me into the parlor. My sister and her husband were almost physically unable to speak. There were hugs, thank-yous, and then I listened as the door closed. The silence was immediately unbearable.

I stood for a moment to see the surroundings. There were flowers around the walls and chairs throughout the parlor. Mr. Baron left on the lamp by the head of the coffin. There were no other lights in the room and no windows to the outside world. I took a moment to look anywhere except at the little girl. Eventually I had to turn. I was struck by her brightness. Her pink dress and blonde hair. She was like a doll in a baby bed, resting, ready to play when the time arrives. She was at peace, her little lungs empty, her hair perfect around her face. I checked my watch. There was no music, no sound from outside the walls, there seemed to be no one left in the entire world.

I moved a big chair next to the coffin and sat down. I was surprised to feel tired, relaxed, even comfortable. In a short time my mind floated between sleep and wakefulness. Dreams flowed like crystal water up and around the smooth stones on the bottom of a river. For the first time in a very long time I didn't feel alone. The warmth of this feeling blended with the natural current of the steady stream of dream scenes, all peaceful. And I lost track of the time, and place, and the big empty room with no windows or ticking clock.

I awoke on top of the tiny child in the coffin, balled up with my face against her face. Seconds passed as I tried to gather my situation. As it became clear where I was, my mind stood still.

Is there anyone else in the room?

What time is it? Is this real?

Why is my hand under her dress? How

could this happen?

I lifted my head slowly and rolled my neck towards the door. Mr. Baron stood in the doorway with horror in his eyes. He ran, and I heard his voice on the phone, "Please, send the police, please hurry, yes, yes," and then silence again.

I climbed from the coffin and straightened my clothes. I crossed my niece's hands in her lap as they had been before. The police wouldn't listen to me. My own sister believed the lies. The Judge sat like a big idiot and listened to my explanation before he sent me to this prison. Someday, hopefully soon, everyone will figure out that it was just a big misunderstanding. What else could it be?

•

I kept the pages in my pocket for a long time before dropping them in the file. I watched the faces of the men I would pass in the hall or sit next to at lunch. They say that some child molesters are geniuses, planning and rationalizing the things they do. Could one of these men have written such a thing? I never found out. I'll never know. I read the story a hundred times and thought about how I would have passed by those folded papers on the city street, but in here I picked them up.

It is easy to make enemies in here. Unlike the enemies on the outside who spread nasty rumors or refuse to say hello in the grocery store, the enemies in here will kill you over nothing. God never intended so many people to live in such a small space.

My friend John makes enemies. He just won't do the little things it takes to blend in and avoid unnecessary confrontations with angry sons-of-bitches like John Wesley Hamilton. Everyone here is under pressure. The pressure of being controlled, and overcrowded, and the pressure which can only come from the instinct of survival. The slightest word, a bump in the hallway, some sideways glance, can set off explosions of extreme violence. Yesterday I saw it happen.

We were standing in the lunch line with our trays in a row. I was ahead of John and he was ahead of John Wesley Hamilton. Mr. Hamilton's arms are as big around as my head and tattoos crisscross his body in faded reds and blacks and greens. He is a man worth fearing.

There was only one bread roll left. I didn't want it. John took it. John Wesley Hamilton apparently likes bread rolls.

"I want that fuckin' roll," he said.

John answered without thinking, "Everybody wants something."

In one instant John Wesley Hamilton, with both hands tight on the tray, swung his body and his arms and the tray from his waist upward with brutal force until the edge of the tray crashed into John's forehead and sent him backwards like a child. Food from both trays flew through the air and blood was immediate and red. John was unconscious before he landed on the ground and his head flopped like a doll's head and popped back on the hard floor bleeding again. His hands rested at his sides and my first clear thought was John is dead.

John Wesley Hamilton stood over the body on the floor still holding the tray. Guards came from all directions. There was yelling and screaming, people pushing. They emptied the cafeteria as a usual precaution, trying to head off a riot or more fights. John was taken to the infirmary. He didn't die. John Wesley Hamilton didn't go down without a fight. He bloodied the nose of a fat guard right before the pepper spray caught him in the face. Still the big man didn't go quietly. As they dragged him out the door, the last guard turned to me and said, "Black, clean up the mess."

Everyone else was gone. There was total silence. Total. Maybe the contrast creates an exaggeration. I remembered once in high school when I found myself alone in the gymnasium after a basketball game. The crowd had been deafening, people everywhere, maximum awareness with senses on overload, and then, in just a few moments, total silence. The sound of a ball bounced one time on the hardwood floor echoing through the gym.

I got down on my knees in the cafeteria. The spot where John's head had rested was a smeared pool of dark blood. Almost black. There was a piece of fried chicken, and scattered crowder peas, a mess of food, and the roll.

That stupid roll. All alone, away from the chicken, and crowder peas, and blood. Off to the side almost like it was ashamed. It made me think again about being a kid. About standing in lunchroom lines, served by ladies with hairnets. About boys getting in stupid fights over stupid things like rolls.

I sat in that cafeteria alone wallowing in the quiet. I didn't realize how much I missed being silently alone. This place is full of noise. Hard noises and constant sounds. It is full of people, angry people and people afraid, but always people, one after the other, crowded in rooms and herded like cattle from place to place. I sat down in that cafeteria and closed my eyes and felt God in the silence. I stayed there until they made me leave.

Rebecca Darby

After a number of years I became eligible for work detail. I pushed and shoved my way to the front of the line so I could grab a window seat on the bus. I didn't want to miss a thing. Nothing. Not a blade of grass, or a dog in the yard, or an old lady sipping tea on the porch. It all flew by so fast. I had to force my mind to stop on those things that seemed the most important.

Her name was Rebecca Darby. It was written in neat black letters on a small white wooden cross on the side of the highway between the prison and our work site. There were fresh flowers at the base of the cross which was nailed to the bottom of a thin pine tree. I never met her. I never even knew she existed until I saw the cross.

The name stuck in my head. Rebecca Darby. Not a strange name, a normal name. The kind of name we can pass by, just like the cross on the side of the road. But no name stands alone. Rebecca Darby must have been surrounded by life. Her name and her cross hold a special place for the people who loved her. There is a mother who carried a baby without a name for nine months and then spread herself on a hospital table to push this baby into a big world. There is a man who touched the belly of the mother of his child and felt it move, so close under the skin. There is a sister who waited in the hospital with grandparents until there was a baby to hold and a name for that baby: Rebecca Darby.

Little Rebecca Darby. That kid down the street with freckles and a smile that stretched forever. That girl who sat in front of the mirror and watched herself grow into a young woman. And that young woman who began to find herself through the teenage years of her journey.

That Saturday morning was like any other Saturday morning. Rebecca Darby woke up next to her husband and touched him gently on the face before she went upstairs to wake the boys. She smiled at the white kitten stretched out on the pillow and sat on the edge of the bed for a few minutes watching them sleep.

There was no time to cry. There was only the sound of tires sliding sideways on a wet highway. The sound of metal and glass in the night air slammed into trees, and the gentle silence of Rebecca Darby leaving this life. And on that place rests a white wooden cross with her name in neat black letters. And under that cross her people come and put fresh flowers and remember the things which give meaning to her name.

•

For every mile of the rest of that day's bus ride I couldn't stop thinking about her, whoever she was. I remembered a day long ago on a boat a few hundred yards off the beach in the Gulf of Mexico fishing for bluefish. Coming from the direction of land I saw something small just above the surface of the water. It was a butterfly. Black with an orange spot on each wing. It flew slowly past me and I watched it going outward across the endless water. It seemed certain of the direction. Not lost, or off course, but certain. How far can a butterfly go? How far out until it can't make it back to dry land? And what happens when the butterfly just can't make it home, like Rebecca Darby just didn't make it home that day? I am thankful for the chance to wonder.

I have read books of theology. I have read books of the history of religion. But I guess the real evidence of the existence of God in those books is my existence itself, the existence of a human being. People want to draw a dark line down the middle of the page at evolution. They write that the definition of a Christian is the belief in Adam and Eve, and the definition of a nonbeliever is the person who has allowed the science of Darwinism to creep inside him and rot his soul. It isn't that easy. Or maybe it isn't that complicated.

If I were God, I would use time to create my most wonderful creation, a person. Time is the most powerful force that exists. It can create and destroy in the blink of a billion evolutionary years. Like a sculptor it can shape and patiently mold.

If I were God I would want my mirror-image to be perfect. I would want my children to have all the tools of survival and wisdom that can only come from their experience in the framework of time. I would want to experiment with other lesser animals and plants, setting in motion a slow hand to craft and shape, using the lessons of success and failure, the knowledge of survival in a changing world, and the integrity of evolution to ultimately produce my children.

God is in no hurry. It isn't a coincidence that the Earth, the oceans, and other animals and plants existed before we did. It isn't a coincidence that we don't have the largest claws, the biggest teeth, or the fastest feet. Instead, we have a soul and a mind. And our soul and mind in this life are wrapped inside a body made perfect through the pressure and balance of a tool called time. A tool used by God to create the men who wrote the Bible, and the men who didn't. Survival is more than coincidence.

There is no line down the middle of the page. People want the world to be simple so they look for differences to separate and simplify. The battleground of evolution and Adam and Eve is bullshit. Same God, same idea, same tool. Only God could use time, and only time could make a person, any person.

I look for connections between our natural instincts of survival and our long-held religious beliefs. I watched a show on television, studies done of the female body. The scientific world has known forever that a man's instincts to spread his seed are powerful and pull crossways with our religious beliefs of marriage and monogamy. But now the studies done on the female reproductive system provide definitive proof that the female body itself works in that same opposite direction.

It seems that when a woman is having sex with the same man over a period of time, her husband, the woman's body identifies this man's sperm. If new sperm from a strange and different man is introduced into the woman's body, the woman's body will repeatedly choose this strange and different sperm over the sperm of her husband to fertilize the egg. Her reproductive parts will actually choose the sperm of the adulterer, the rapist, over the sperm of the man who may have a history of providing for and protecting and fathering her other children. Now I ask, if I work hard every day to support my wife and children, and I am faithful, and loving, and honest, why would God cause my wife's internal organs to purposefully choose the sperm of the man who rapes her in our home while I'm at work? What kind of God decides my wife should bear the child of her immoral lover instead of the child of her husband, even when our sperm stands side by side at the egg temple? Or does it have nothing whatsoever to do with God?

Now what do we do with this piece of information? On which side of the line does it fall? Our bodies don't seem to care about our little religious and historical institutions of marriage and monogamy. Our bodies have an animal instinct for the species to survive despite ourselves. Does that come from Adam and Eve, or does that come from a billion years of the lessons of survival? Should we pretend the scientific test results don't exist? Or should we just draw another solid line down the middle of the page?

letters to Janie (6th letter)

Dear Janie,

You can call it giving up, or you can call it recognizing reality, but I have reached a place in my journey where you don't matter. You'll probably say that if I had truly reached such a place, I wouldn't need to write you a letter to say so. Why write a letter to a person who doesn't matter? Well, because the letter isn't for you, it's for me.

If you're still alive, you're middle-aged, a little extra weight around the middle, dark rings under your tired eyes. Don't worry, I get no pleasure from it. Where would the pleasure be? I once thought that simply having a vagina would be enough to survive in this world. Not just survive, but have the world by the tail. I don't see it now. How is your prison any better than mine? A person with multiple personality disorder, a schizophrenic, has lots of people in one mind. What do they call a person who doesn't have anyone in his mind? Nobody at all.

It would be a shock to get something back from you. To know you were getting my letters, or not getting my letters, or getting pissed off, or not getting pissed off, or living a happy life under a rock, or dead, or eaten up with syphilis, or shoveling hot piles of shit in a cave in Hell with the Devil looking over your shoulder. God, I'd probably do it again. Stand there and take the gun out of your hand, sit down and watch the blood soak into the brown carpet, making it darker brown.

Wait for fate to arrive and haul my ass to jail. I sit here 18 years later, and I'd probably do it all again for you. What does that make me? It makes me Gabriel Black. And you can't change that.

Sincerely,

Gabriel Black

a vacation

Carl Anderson had some LSD smuggled in last week. For the right price you can get almost anything in here. You can even place orders with people like Carl who will find a way. The law of supply and demand exists in every little dark corner of the world.

I took two tabs of LSD (or whatever the hell it was) along with some prison-made clear alcohol that tasted like turpentine. When I woke up the next day in the infirmary there were bruises all over my forearms and a gash under my left eye. Later, back in my cell, I found two pages in my handwriting folded in my shoe. I have no memory of writing these sentences, but I haven't changed a word.

Let me outta here
Let me the fuck outta here
I can eat my hand and slowly shit myself out
and down the toilet and through the pipes to the
sewage pools floating under the clear blue sky
on the other side of these walls.
The ugly old voodoo woman with the long gray
hair leads me around the house - extortion is the
purest form of flattery—the means utilized
by a person who wants something from a person
who has something.
The extorter covets
the victim possesses
without the inequity
the act itself would not exist

or have a reason to exist
like a beaver hole,
What could possibly be the point of a baby face down
in a puddle outside a whorehouse?
What could possibly justify the brilliance of the hands
of the woman at the piano, knowing where to go before
the mind has enough time to send the message?
Let me the fuck outta here
Let me go. I didn't kill anybody.
I don't belong here, with these people, in this
asshole of the Universe.
If I scratch my fingernails against the wall, in
the same place, for 20 years, will there be a
hole in the crust for me to crawl through, and
if there is, will there be anything left of me to
lie on a beach and extort what is rightfully
mine from the pointy-headed bureaucrats and the
skinless politicians with their firm little faces
squeezed like cookie dough in the cracks of
the asses of the fourth generation businessman
who lives a hundred years later off the raw
genius of a dead relative who was not afraid
to be proud of himself or even other men who
are better than other men?
In a world of six billion people can I
just slip through the cracks and be sent to
live in a little house, maybe in Colorado, with
a woman who touches me when I sleep, and
a boy who looks up at me and asks how to
get a fish off a hook and a baby who cries and I don't care,
and a job?

Let me feel the pain in my back from carrying a
load too heavy
the blisters on my hands
a good night's sleep my body needs
or if I can't have it, say so
Just say it —
"Gabriel Black, you can't have it"
"You can't have any of it"
"I don't care if you didn't murder the man"
"I don't care what you deserve in this life"
"Come into my arms and let me hold you for
a weightless eternity, in Heaven, but you won't
have anything in this life. Not one damned
thing, so stop asking, and stop begging, and see
if you can scrape up some little crumb
of evidence that I exist for your pitiful little
file and remember that you are me"

•

The last sections in quotation marks were not in my
handwriting. The letters were long and slender in a bluer
ink. The margins were perfect.

forgiveness

I was taught that my sins are forgiven through confession. Leon believes you can get forgiveness beforehand. I hate to say it, but Leon is a more interesting person since he had that stroke. If you can put up with his obsession with killing flies, the stroke seems to have uncovered a part of his mind worth exploring.

"Leon, what did you ever do to end up here?"

Leon watched a fly land on the wall out of his reach. As he spoke to me his eyes never left the nasty little creature washing its wings.

"I killed folks."

"How many folks?"

"Two folks."

He answered my questions without suspicion or hesitation. The answers were childlike, but answers a child could never give.

"Who were they, Leon?"

"One was my momma."

"Who was the other?"

"A white man named Clay Bolger."

The fly left its spot on the gray wall and flew up towards the light, took one pass around by the bed, and stopped silent on the cover of Leon's Bible.

"You worried about going to Hell, Leon?"

The wheelchair inched forward towards the fly on the Bible. Leon's right arm lifted slowly as his left arm controlled the roll of the chair. Suddenly, and a lot faster than you would think the old man could move, the swatter came down dead on target. The fat fingers of Leon

Evers retrieved the fly to add to the collection.

He turned to me and said, "I ain't goin' to no Hell."

"How do you know that, Leon?"

His eyes began to search again.

"I know because before I killed them people, I asked the Lord to forgive me for what I was 'bout to do. And the Lord put his hand on my shoulder and he said, 'Leon, I forgive you.'"

John was in the room. He waited a few moments of silence and said, "Well, Leon, I guess under your set of rules, nobody's goin' to Hell."

Leon took his eyes from the window and turned to John. He said, "Hell's full of people who didn't ask first."

"So all you've got to do is ask?"

Leon smiled, "That's it."

"So once God gave you forgiveness beforehand, you could do whatever you wanted?"

"That's it."

John asked, "So what did you do?"

Leon caught the glimpse of the flight of a fly across the bars of the cell. His head turned as the fly stopped in a spot near the far top corner of the room.

"I cut that man's head off with one swing of the ax and when my momma yelled, the second swing crushed her skull."

It was a green fly, and he seemed to know he'd come to the wrong cell. The fly watched us out of the side of that little green fly eye, a prize in any collection.

Maybe it seems unnatural not to ask the man why he killed his mother and that white man, but in prison, nobody asks why.

John told a story:

"When I was in high school, about the eleventh grade, I had a huge crush on a girl named Melanie Figures. Jesus, she was pretty. I can see her now, in the gym, with her hair in a ponytail, smiling.

"I wanted to ask her out, but every time I got near her I forgot what to say. I could practice, and plan, and even make notes, but when she picked up on the other end of the phone, or I saw her in the hall, I couldn't remember anything. Her eyes were calm. She was always nice to me.

"I finally asked her out, and she said yes. Her house was at the end of a long, curving driveway. I spent about two hours trying to make my hair look right, and then I borrowed my brother's car.

"I turned off the road and headed down the driveway. From out of the bushes jumped a cat. There was no time to stop. It was just there, in a split second, and I hit it. I killed it.

"Jesus, I can remember it like it happened yesterday. I knew it was her cat. It was a big orange cat she talked about called Sugar. She had told me she had the cat since she was a baby. And there I was, stopped in her driveway, just a few trees and bushes between me and the girl's front door, with Sugar under the car.

"My mind raced from one option to the other. Do I go to the door and tell her the truth? Do I tell her I found the cat in the road after someone else killed it? Either way our date would be over. She'd be crying all night, and maybe even longer.

"So I picked up the bloody cat by its tail, opened the trunk of the car, and dropped it in. I figured I'd get rid of it in the woods the next day and she'd just think the cat ran away. We could have our date, live happily ever after, and no one would need to know. It was the fuckin' cat's fault anyway. When I looked up at the house I saw Melanie looking down at me from the upstairs window as I closed the trunk. I knew she was too far away to have seen the cat.

"I was so damned nervous by the time I knocked on the door I don't remember much. We went to the movies and she let me hold her hand. Her fingers were soft and small and she smelled like flowers. We laughed at things that weren't funny, and I felt like I could be with her forever and nothing else would matter.

"As we were leaving the movie theater I went to the bathroom, and she asked me for my keys so she could sit in the car and listen to the radio. Two minutes later I was takin' a piss and it dawned on me. I ran half-zipped through the lobby of the theater and out the door into the parking lot. She stood at the back of the car, trunk open, lookin' inside. Why was she in the trunk? Why? She must have been thinking about it since we left her house.

"There was nothing I could do. There was no explanation. She wouldn't even let me drive her home. She never talked to me again. Not a word.

"Not one word."

The green fly left the corner of the cell in a slow flight directly towards Leon Evers in his wheelchair. The Fly Man raised his hand and took a mighty swing at the creature. I pictured the ax raised above his head coming down into the skull of his mother. And then the fly was gone.

my brother

It is strange to say, but I only have one clear memory of my brother, Johnny. He was nineteen, and I had just turned twelve. It was past midnight, and we were sitting on the front porch. Our parents were asleep. The lights in the house were all out, but we could see each other by the streetlight. It was raining.

Johnny held a pistol in his lap. He wouldn't tell me where it came from. It was black. Johnny left me on the porch as he walked around the neighborhood circling behind the Woodwards' house, through the vacant lot, down by Missy Lambert's garage, and back home. I knew where he went because I followed him, stepping barefoot through the wet grass in the shadows. Our hair was wet.

I got back to the porch before Johnny.

"Where'd you go?" I asked.

"Nowhere."

"Why you got that gun, Johnny?"

"If you tell Dad I'll shoot you in the balls."

After a few minutes Johnny set out again to roam through the neighborhood. It never occurred to me to tell Dad. I wouldn't have told him even if Johnny hadn't threatened to shoot me in the balls. He was my brother.

Throughout my childhood it seems he was in and out of the house. I don't know where he would go when he wasn't with us. My father and Johnny couldn't be in the same room at the same time without words or fists. My mother was always between them, forced to choose, without ever choosing at all, and forced to walk the line between mother and wife. I can still see the look on my momma's face when my daddy would be drunk and Johnny would stand up silent, prepared to take a beating. But somehow, I can't remember the look on my brother's face.

I really didn't know him at all. I am left with just one clear image. From that I try to understand him. The image of Johnny, standing in the rain, holding that black pistol at his side, hair wet, blue jeans soaked against his legs, barefooted.

"What are you doing, Johnny?" I needed to know.

He looked at me like he'd forgotten I was there and whispered, "You can't help me."

I don't know whether I should be thankful to God for giving me this one clear memory, and perhaps taking away the others, or whether I should be angry. I would like to have known my brother. I could use him now. Many times I go back to that one memory, replaying parts over and over, looking for something I hadn't noticed before, something to make my brother more alive.

We sat on the porch for a long time without speaking. Johnny rubbed his head and wiped the gun back and forth on a leg of his pants.

After a long time Johnny turned to me and said, "Gabe, I don't expect you to understand, but tonight was the last night. If I stay here, I'll end up killin' the son-of-a-bitch, and that ain't right for Momma. It ain't right for you."

"Where you gonna go?" I asked.

He was crying. He didn't want me to see, but he was crying. My brother John stood up, walked down the front porch steps in the rain, and I never saw him again. Ever.

After some of the pain had gone away my mother used to tell stories about Johnny. She would smile when she spoke his name. It's funny though, I can't remember a single story. Not one.

I found a book called *The Diving Bell and the Butterfly* written by a Frenchman named Jean-Dominique Bauby. The man was healthy, married, with children, and a good job. One day, out of the blue, he had some type of stroke in his brain stem. The man literally woke up a few weeks later in the hospital completely paralyzed. He couldn't speak, he couldn't move, he couldn't even swallow. His only form of communication was blinking his one good eye. Mr. Bauby wrote his book by blinking letters and having someone transcribe his words.

I couldn't help comparing his prison with mine. We both lost our freedom and human independence. Neither of us deserved our condition, although I brought mine on myself and he was just struck down seemingly at random. Our walls are different, but walls just the same.

His situation is worse. Not just because he physically cannot walk, or talk, or taste food, but because he has no option of suicide. None. He does not have the choice to end his own agony. Whether he would choose suicide is not the issue. God did not give Jean-Dominique Bauby any input. He was force-fed, his ass wiped like a baby, and left at the window strapped to his wheelchair to see the things he could not have. His mind was left intact as an extra punishment.

Please do not bury me in a coffin. There were ancient Indians who believed that a person's soul doesn't slip from their bodies until three or four days after they die. What if this is true and all those souls are trapped underground in those airtight metal coffins? What if they can't get out to go to the places they're supposed to go, screaming and kicking down there? Jean-Dominique Bauby died only a few weeks after his book was published. Because he didn't have the option to kill himself, I got the chance to read a book written by a man who had nothing but the wink of his eye to communicate how it felt to be on such a strange journey.

Carl

What possible evidence of God exists in Crazy Carl Anderson?

I've asked myself that question many times. It isn't an easy question to answer, but I decided it was worth the time to think about it.

Nobody likes to be assigned to the cell of Carl Anderson. There's a reason. On a regular basis, Carl wakes up in the middle of the night, staggers over half-asleep to the other bunk, and pisses all over his sleeping cellmate. It always seems to happen during the first few nights some new kid has been moved into the cell.

We'll wait for the yell. The new guy jumps up wiping himself and cussing. Carl finishes his business and crawls back into bed. He got the shit beaten out of him more than once, but it doesn't seem to make a difference.

•

One day in the yard Carl whispered, "Hey, Gabe, you wanna smoke a joint?"

Knowing Carl, I knew he probably actually had a joint.

I said, "We're standing in the middle of the yard. I don't think this would be a good place to smoke a joint."

It was winter, and we had the collars of our coats turned up.

Carl whispered, "Why not?"

"Well, Carl, because there are guards all around the yard, and snitches, and we'll get caught. That's why not."

Carl giggled to himself and said, "There's a fifty-fifty chance you'll get caught no matter what."

I tried not to treat him like an idiot.

"What?"

"Just what I said. No matter where you are, when you smoke the weed, there's a fifty-fifty chance you'll get caught."

It was hard for me to believe that Carl actually believed such a thing.

"So, Carl, you think that there's the same chance of getting caught smoking weed if you're standing alone in the middle of the desert a hundred miles from another human being, or if you're standing in the middle of a prison yard with prison guards all around? Is that what you're saying?"

"It's fifty-fifty."

"No Carl, it's not fifty-fifty. The guy out in the desert probably won't ever get caught, and if we smoke a joint right here, we'll probably get caught every time."

Carl pulled a little white nub of the end of a joint from his coat pocket and put it between his lips. He struck a match and cupped it around his mouth. There was the faint, sweet smell of marijuana.

Carl said, "Where's a guy in the desert gonna get weed anyway?"

I realized that Carl Anderson had created another reality for himself. It was just as real as my reality, and maybe a little nicer. He had an imaginary girlfriend who sent him envelopes full of pubic hair. In Carl's world a person stands an equal chance of being caught smoking pot on the moon or in front of his mother. And he pisses on his roommate.

•

I was sitting with Carl the day he found out he was granted parole.

"Holy shit! Holy shit! I'm gettin' outta here. I'm goin' home."

And then Carl stopped on the word "home." He just stopped like a clock on its last tick, no warning, and stared at his hands. It was a trigger, the word "home," which seemed to set in motion the slow turn of his reality. Only God and Carl knew what horrible things happened to him at home, and only God could give Carl a new place to go inside his mind.

They had to literally drag the man from his cell on the day he was released. Carl fought like a run-over dog, biting and screaming. It took four guards and a can of pepper spray to get him outside to freedom.

Through a window I could see Crazy Carl Anderson standing on the other side of the fence, bloody and small. He tried to crawl back over, and they had to cut him out of the razor wire. His hands looked like balls of raw meat. I never saw him again after that day.

sounds

In this place we forget the stillness of silence. It exists in rare, short moments sometimes years apart. Since I've been here I could count these moments on my hands and tell when and where each took place. I had one this morning, sitting in the yard near the farthest corner, alone, on a clear, cool October morning. Quiet spread out unexpectedly like a white sheet floating down from the sky, and I closed my eyes. There was one sound, a mockingbird singing, not too far away, the pitch and roll of the sharp notes alone in the still air, with time to hear each sound separate and transparent.

It made me search my memory for the sounds in my life, important sounds that stand apart and can still make me feel the way I felt when I heard them for the first time.

•

(#1) When I was a boy I spent a few summers with my Uncle Hugh. He was big and hard and owned horses. Uncle Hugh's wife, Aunt Betty, was a strong country woman. They didn't have any children, and they didn't want any. I think they took me those summers out of a blood obligation to get me out of my daddy's house for a while.

The horses were fascinating. Heavy animals with soft eyes. I spent as much time with them as I could. My favorite was named Misty, and Uncle Hugh taught me how to brush her and saddle and ride. One morning Misty wasn't with the other horses. I walked through the field past the fishpond to the other side of the tree line. There was a sound. I stopped and listened. Again. Dull and hollow, a pounding, every four or five seconds, and then I saw Misty. I ran to her. The horse was wedged between the barbed-wire fence and a big oak tree. Her front hoof was caught in the root and somehow bent under and around the bottom strand of wire. Her side was torn in strips and then there was the sound again. The horse swung her head from right to left hard against the trunk of the tree, and again, and again, in frustration, and fear, wrapped inside the pain and agony of spending the night trapped, with barbs burying themselves in her flesh and the wire tightening around the bottom leg.

I ran. I ran through the field, and past the fishpond, with that sound echoing and the image of the horse's face, mangled and swollen, being carved in my childhood memory step by step.

(#2) My mother crying. The soft sound that I would hear too many times lying awake in bed when I was a boy. Sometimes she would come and sit in my room in the dark and I would fake sleep. I used to believe that she came to my room because it was a place she didn't think my father would come after her. Later I learned she never came to my room until she was sure he was either far away or fast asleep.

The violence of the sound from the horse's head clashes with the muted sadness of my mother at night, but they both rise from the same immovable frustration. The sound of my mother crying made me feel more worthless and alone than any sound in my life, yet I wish I could hear it one more time just to know she was in the room next to me.

(#3) I can hear the sharp, exact sound of Janie's gun firing the first bullet. It's loud in my memory and the concussion shakes loose images. I remember seeing the gun, and seeing her finger pull the trigger, and being amazed at the loudness.

(#4) After the trial, and the Judge's sentence, I was transported from the local jail to the penitentiary. During the months I spent in the local jail I listened to stories about prison, but nothing can prepare a man for the sound of the prison door closing behind him. The heavy, iron vibration slams shut with finality, a period at the end of a man's real life. I specifically remember knowing that this sound would be one I would always remember.

(#5) And now I sit and think about the song of the mockingbird this morning. Good or bad, I will no longer take for granted such simple pleasures. I cannot change things, so I have to understand them.

the weatherlady

I remember walking into a bar in New Orleans. It was before I met Janie. There was a woman on the other side of the room sitting with friends. At the instant our eyes met I felt that feeling. It's like some kind of chemical released in my head. We smiled, stared a moment too long several times, back and forth, and then she left. We never spoke.

She was blonde, wearing a green dress, with just the right balance of nasty and ladylike. There's no reason I should remember her, but I miss that little feeling. It doesn't exist in here. There's no sense of attraction, no face to look for in the crowd, no chance for casual flirtation. Except, of course, the weatherlady.

She's on channel 22, everyday, bright and happy and talking just to me like I was the only person in the whole damn world who cares about the weather. Her name is Penny Tate. She smiles and points and tells me what's going to happen tomorrow in St. Paul, Minnesota, and Portland, Oregon. She's a good Catholic girl, strong hips and stout breasts. There's a twinkle in her eye. Sometimes I can almost convince myself that I love her. How much do you have to know about a woman to love her? I know her work schedule. I know her dresses, and her jewelry, and the way she walks.

"Black! Change the fuckin' channel."

I can imagine Penny Tate at the door when I pick her up for our first date. She loves me, finds me interesting. She wants to get married and doesn't try to hide the way she feels. Sometimes she even lets me kiss her on the mouth at a restaurant. And Penny wants kids, Penny Black, lots of kids. She quits her job. It wasn't important to her anyway. She says she felt silly up there.

"Turn on the game, freak, channel 12. Why you always watchin' the weather? Who gives a shit about the weather? It's always the same in here."

I beg for rain. I watch the radar screen with the colored storms drifting across our spot on the map. I've tried to believe that I like the rain because it reminds me of my mother making chocolate chip cookies for me when I couldn't go outside. But that's not it. That's not it at all. When it rains, really hard, nobody goes outside. All the free people become prisoners in their homes or offices. And then we're all the same. When a massive hurricane builds up in the Gulf of Mexico and barrels like a howling ball of water onto shore, it equalizes everything. We're all human beings again. The hurricane doesn't care.

Penny Tate changes her voice and becomes serious as she tells me about the sustained wind speed east of the eye of the hurricane. I think she will be a great mother for our little boy. She's never actually been in a hurricane. I can tell by the way she's gotten caught up in the fear. Penny projects landfall by tomorrow morning, and I let myself imagine the mighty winds will blow down the walls of this prison, destroy all the houses and buildings, and wipe the slate clean like the Yankees burning their way through the South. All court records will be lost in the flood along with birth certificates and Social Security numbers and credit reports. Penny and I will get a fresh start out there in Colorado, in the mountains.

"If you don't change the channel I'm gonna split your fuckin' head open."

Penny looks down at me and says, "Take all necessary precautions. Stock up on bottled water and batteries. Remove items from your yard that can be blown by the wind through your windows. And Gabriel Black, God willing, I'll see you tomorrow."

I can't wait.

The rage his face brings is more than I am able to control. No matter how many times he is resurrected, I can bash in his skull with a shovel again and again. There is no morality or law with the strength to freeze my hands on the backswing, the shovel sliding through air on its way to his head. There is no divine intervention or pangs of regret to slow down the rusted metal shovelhead as it picks up speed. And there is no sympathy when his fat little head explodes like a watermelon suspended in midair, slammed with a baseball bat, tiny bits of black blood flying in all directions, some landing quietly on the skin of my face and arms.

Even in hindsight I cannot gather the energy to hide evidence or wait for the opportunity when no one else is around. The rage his face brings is more than I can control. I have never killed before. Not even a bird. He falls to his hands and knees, his hair a thick bloody mess. Coughing, probably paralyzed by pain, borderline conscious, maybe even childlike already.

The pause between the first blow and the second is only a result of the physical reality of the time it takes to raise the shovel above my head. I know exactly what I am doing. There can be no other purpose to my actions. There can be no other result. I have seen what a shovel can do in the field. It reaches its peak above my head, for an instant still, like a statue, the artistic side of intentional murder. Gravity adds a few extra miles per hour to the shovelhead as it speeds towards home. My emotions remain clean, free of the burdens of empathy and salvation, as the metal stings the skull.

His arms instantly lose the ability to hold his body from the floor. He lets go in a sprawl, face down, spread out like spilled paint, lifeless and oozing, the shovel broken, the wooden handle still in my hand. Almost immediately there is relief. Immediately I can weigh the fact that I would rather spend the rest of my life in this prison knowing he is dead than have the chance to be free and carry the knowledge that he is in the world. I prefer my rage to be focused.

It feels like I'm floating.

I wonder if this is the way God feels when He exacts His revenge?

my mother and my son

My mother and my unborn son were the only two people in this life who were true reflections of what I believe
God to be. I don't pretend my mother didn't have her
faults. But the memory of her can make me feel like I
hope to feel in Heaven when I can sit with my boy on my
knee.

Every night when I was a child my mother would
kneel next to me at the edge of the bed and have me say
a prayer. We would say it together with my hands folded
and my eyes closed.

"Now I lay me down to sleep, I pray the Lord my
soul to keep.

If I should die before I wake, I pray the Lord my soul
to take."

"Mom."

"Yes, Gabriel."

"Is God in charge of showing me the things I see
every day?"

"Yes, I believe He is."

"Today, walking home from the bus stop, I saw a red
bird."

Mom asked, "Was it pretty?"

"It was dead on the side of the road. There were ants
on his feathers."

She had her arm around me and gave a little
squeeze.

I asked, "Why would God show me something so

pretty, so red, but make it be dead? I wanted to hold it, to touch it, but it looked sad. His eye was open."

My mom was always very patient. I wonder if she imagined I would remember her words so many years later?

"Don't be sad. By the time you saw it, that red bird was already in Heaven. At the moment he died, his spirit flew up to the clouds higher than he could ever fly when he was alive. God just gave you the chance to see those pretty red feathers before his body goes back to the Earth."

Her voice was calm and sure.

"Gabriel, one day, a long time from now, your time will come, and you'll go to Heaven, too. I promise. And when you get there, you'll see me, and that red bird, and everybody and everything else you love. I promise."

•

I never had the chance to sit by the side of a little bed and teach my own son the prayer my mother taught me. And I never had the chance to explain to him about red birds, and Heaven, and promises. I wonder sometimes if I could have been half the parent my mother was to me, but that doesn't matter. I don't think anymore about the twenty years I didn't get to spend with my son. I only think about the months he was inside of Janie, just below the surface on the other side of my hand.

It doesn't matter that I never saw his tiny face, or held him in my arms. It's like my mother used to tell me. There's no in-between. I either believe or I don't believe, and I choose to believe. The alternative is nothing. The alternative is to know my baby died because his mother swam in the Devil's broth and wanted him dead. The alternative is to know I did nothing to protect my only child.

•

"Daddy."

"Yes."

"Tell me the story again about Grandma and the red bird."

"Well I just told you that story last night."

"I know, Daddy, but it's my favorite. When you tell it, you sound different. It makes me think of Grandma's picture. I wish she could've waited to go to Heaven until after I was born so I could know her. I wish I could've heard Grandma tell the story herself."

His name is John Thomas. I named him after my brother. I put my arm around him and say, "She'll wait for you where she is, and you'll come to her."

John Thomas kneels at the side of the bed and puts his hands together.

"Now I lay me down to sleep, I pray the Lord my soul to keep.

If I should die before I wake, I pray the Lord my soul to take.

And please ask Grandma to wait. I won't be long."

the best day of your life

Everybody has a best day, one, single, very best day of their whole life. I look around at the people in this place. Even these people, the outcasts, society's garbage, cripples, fags, immoral shit eaters. Even these people, every one of them, had a best day. One day that stands apart.

•

"Is there one day, Leon, that you can remember as your best day? The best day of your life?"

"That would be the day my baby girl was born."

Leon smiled. I could tell he was seeing something in his mind.

"Boy, I was proud. I never been so proud of nothin' in my life. They handed me that baby, all wrapped in a blanket. I didn't think nothin' about the bad things I did in my life. I didn't think nothin' about all the bad things that could happen to my baby in this world."

John asked, "What was her name?"

The different voice snapped Leon back to where we were.

"Lida Mae Evers."

"What happened to her?" I asked.

Leon looked up slow and said, "It don't matter what happened to her. You asked me what was the best day of my life. It don't have nothin' to do with the day before, or the day after. It was the best day because how I felt, and how that baby looked."

Leon's mind drifted back and the smile formed again.

"I held her, and I just started cryin'. No reason.

151

Didn't need no reason. I just started cryin'. Cryin' and smilin' at the same time. Kinda like when it rains with the sun shinin'."

Leon stopped talking and just laughed to himself. His body bobbed up and down in the wheelchair while he remembered the very best day of his life.

"What's your best day, John?"

"It hasn't come yet."

"What's that mean?"

"My best day will be the day they let me out of this place. It'll be the day I walk down the hall, and the doors slide open for me, and I walk out through the front gate. Nothin' else will matter. It's like Leon said, it's got nothing to do with the day before or the day after."

"Where you gonna go?" I asked.

"It doesn't matter. There won't be any hugs in the parking lot, or parades, or jobs lined up. I just know it'll be the best day I'll ever have. Sometimes, if I think about it hard enough, I can start to cry the way Leon cried holding his baby."

We all sat quiet for a few minutes.

John said, "Beginnings and ends."

He was on the top bunk, on his back, hands behind his head, looking up at the gray ceiling.

"We spend so much time thinking about beginnings and ends, we don't appreciate the middle. Nobody would ever say their greatest day was some random day in the middle. Some Tuesday in November when you went to work, or took the kids to school, or rolled over on your wife for a few minutes. What would be the fuckin' point?

"It's the beginnings and ends. The first day of

school, the day you quit your job, the last time you saw your wife before she got hit by a truck.

"Or the first time you held your baby. Or the last second, of the last minute, of the last day I will spend in this Godforsaken shit palace."

After a few minutes of no talking, John rolled over and looked down at me in the chair below. He said, "Sorry."

I have become a man with no beginnings and no ends.

Janie,

This is the last letter I will write to you. I wish I could say I've reached the promised land of indifference, but it would be a lie. I wish I could say I don't hate you, or love you, or think about you at all, but I can't say that. It wouldn't be human.

I have so much time to think about things. Too much. I still remember lying in bed with you our last night. Turning on the light while you slept. Tracing the long scar down your brown back with my finger. Stopping, just for a moment, and wondering if it might be best to take your head in my hands and snap your fuck-ing neck with all my might. Quick, painless, with a low almost nonexistent popping sound in your spine, and your last breath, cut short, trapped inside your sick body. I would do it now, right now, if I had the chance. But I won't get the chance, and we won't have to know for sure.

Instead, this is the last letter I need to send. It doesn't matter that you may not have received any of the letters before. It doesn't matter that I couldn't accomplish indif-ference. I've been able to narrow down the things in this life that really do matter. And you're not one of them. If it hadn't been you it would have been someone else, some-where else, for some other reason.

But then I think to myself, what if you got pregnant again that last night we were together? What if you've been trying to see me all these years, and they won't let you? You've been telling our boy about me and he's out there, waiting for the chance to meet his father? And what if gravity crawls up my ass headfirst and the world spins away into everlasting black damnation with a lemon twist? And what if the only thing I ever did right in this life was to go to prison so you wouldn't have to?

Goodbye Janie Fitzpatrick. Everything's going to be all right.

Gabriel

little league football

There are some memories like little league football simply not clouded with confusion or questions. I can still smell the cut grass in the fall, somewhere between the summer heat and autumn's cool mornings, huddled together with my teammates at one end of the field watching the other team practice plays at their end. They always seemed huge until the whistle blew and we ran down the field on the opening kickoff to meet the enemy. After the butterflies were gone, they didn't look so big.

Andy Bailey was our quarterback. I wonder what he's doing now? He was just a little bit bigger and a little bit faster than the rest of us. When he called a play in the huddle we shut our mouths and listened. Usually he said something worth saying. He hated to lose almost as much as I did.

I can hear him say, "Gabby, can I get around your end on the bootleg?"

I don't know why he called me Gabby. I didn't talk much. I was small and tough, faster than my limp let me look, and I could catch everything. I was that kid at practice who gets pulverized by the middle linebacker and gets back up and staggers to the huddle. More than once I saw the coaches smile at each other when I acted like it didn't hurt and swallowed hard to stop the tears. It was football, man. I don't remember many scores of games, I just remember being out there and loving every minute of it.

JuJu Mitchell was the fastest kid in town. He was

poor. Poorer than me, though we never really knew the difference. He didn't have any pads in his pants, and he wore his big brother's helmet that was too big. With Andy Bailey and JuJu on the same team, we were tough to beat.

"Yeah, you can get around the corner. Number 86 is crashin' inside every time you pitch to JuJu on the far-side sweep."

I played for seven years, different teams, usually played end on offense and safety on defense. Sometimes the coach would put me at noseguard to shoot the gap around a fat center and try to get in the backfield before the play got going. I was always the dirtiest kid after every game and every practice. I got my teeth kicked in more than once, but somehow I only remember the good parts.

•

The last game I ever played was against a team from the big city. Our coach called it a bowl game and set up all the arrangements. Those boys came to our field in a shiny bus. They had bright red uniforms and socks up to their knees. Scared the holy piss out of me and everybody else. Even Andy Bailey had a look in his eye I hadn't seen before.

Our parents sat in the bleachers and drank cold Coca-Colas. Mr. Greer from the town newspaper even showed up. Me and Andy and JuJu went to the middle of the field for the flip of the coin. Three of those boys stood across from us, their helmets shined in the morning sun. We looked like hound dogs with our mismatched jerseys and hand-me-down equipment. I couldn't wait for the whistle to blow and to get that first lick.

We fought back and forth the whole game. They were big, but slow. JuJu couldn't get past the linebackers. On offense they had some fancy signals, and sometimes they'd change the play at the line. I was playing nose-guard on first and second downs and safety on pass plays. By the third quarter we figured out their fancy signals. We knew where they were going before they got there, but we couldn't move the ball worth a damn. At the end of the third quarter they were ahead 6 to nothing. JuJu finally broke a long one and got down to their twenty-yard line with two minutes to go. They held us on first and second downs, and on third down Andy fumbled the snap but got it back. It was fourth down, twenty yards from home. We hadn't run the bootleg all day.

I said, "Andy, number 54 is crashin' inside on my end. You can bootleg and get the corner."

Andy gave me one look and called the play, "Fake 48 pitch, bootleg left. On one. Break."

I was left end. On the snap I took a step backwards and let that big son-of-a-bitch crash inside. Andy faked the pitch to JuJu on the right-hand sweep and put the ball on his hip. As he made the turn towards the left side I waited for number 54 to realize his mistake before I took him out at the knees. I just remember lying in the grass hearing the crowd scream and catching a glimpse of Andy running down the sidelines for the touchdown. JuJu kicked the extra point to win the game.

I'll never forget it. There's nothing about it I need to figure out or worry about. It's pure, and it's free, and it's mine.

I was lying alone in my bottom bunk, the cell door open, reading a book. I saw that little son-of-a-bitch walk past the door, black as coal, and glance at me. The instincts of a man in prison are like the instincts of an animal. If I had been in some office, at some job, in some nice building, and a man had walked past my office door and looked inside, it might mean nothing. But in here it could mean everything.

Two days earlier I had noticed that same little son-of-a-bitch in the yard watching me. It doesn't matter why, and there's no reason to try to figure it out or fix it. I kept reading my book, the same line over and over, as I reached my hand against the wall and under the mattress to pull my shiv. It was made from the hard plastic handle of a toothbrush, filed to a sharp point, with a handle wrapped fat at the base with tape. I placed the book down on my chest and propped my head high on the pillow like I was falling asleep, eyes closed to a cat slit.

In a few minutes that little son-of-a-bitch peeked his eye around the bottom corner of the cell. The silence was noticeable, and my heart pounded in my chest. He crouched low and edged through the cell door, quiet but clear. My hand tightened on the shiv held next to the far side of my body. I imagined him thinking how easy this was going to be. How lucky he was that this old man had fallen asleep, and how his knife would slide so easily under the ribs with his other hand over my mouth.

He moved up towards the bed. I waited until the exact moment when there would be no turning back for him or me. If it wasn't now it would be tomorrow, or the next day, or the next. My body jerked up and my hand swung all or nothing in a solid half circle ending with the shiv buried to the handle through his shirt and into the little man's side. Mostly I remember his eyes, big and round like the eyes of so many men who have died with violence. His knife hit home in my chest but with a force cut short by the shock of something strange entering his body and the instant recognition of pain and fear. As he stumbled backwards his knife fell to the floor and I was against him, chest against chest, pushing his balance to the opposite wall, my shiv pulled out and thrust again, and then again, and a fourth time into his left side. His bloodshot eyes man to man against mine, rage against forgiveness, and with no sound he died between me and the cold wall, slumping down slowly like he was tired.

And before I could think another thought, I felt envy. Complete and total envy that the bloody little fucker should leave this place, and I should be left here standing over him, praying he was me, and I was him.

I used to believe that the proof of God in suicide was my decision to choose against it every day. Now the circle has turned. Now I know that the option is the gift. We don't condemn the man in physical pain, with incurable cancer, when he takes his own life. But there's pain in this world worse than any physical pain that might wrack this body of mine. God gave us a soul which separates us from all his other creatures. But with the soul comes the capacity to hurt worse than any animal or beast. Not only can we feel this pain, but we can understand it, and put it in words. The understanding sometimes only makes it worse when there's no cure.

•

"I give you my word, every sin will be forgiven
mankind and all the blasphemies men utter,
but whoever blasphemies against the Holy Spirit
will never be forgiven. He carries the guilt of his
sin without end." Mark 3:28-29

•

People in this world say they believe in God and
Heaven. People like the preacher on TV, or the old lady
at home with the Bible in her lap, or the men I see in
prison who turn to God only when there is nowhere else
left to turn. But when it comes down to it, they are afraid
to die. Somewhere in their minds must exist a speck of
doubt, just the tiniest blasphemy, because if there were
no doubt then there would be no fear. No fear of leaving
this life in whatever way and walking with God to wherever He may take us.

There are no more specks of doubt in me. Not only
am I sure as I stand above the dead man in my cell, but I
will rely upon the promise. I have asked myself the question a million times, "If God gives me more than I can
endure, how will I know?" He'll bring me home, that's
how I will know.

the search itself

I was nine years old. My mother's birthday was two weeks away. I clearly remember knowing my father would forget her birthday. I also clearly remember seeing Billy Kendall's mother with a big ring on her finger that sparkled on her hand when she moved. My mother didn't have a ring like that. She didn't have anything pretty, just for her. I decided if Billy Kendall's mother deserved a ring like that, so did my mother. Even bigger.

I mowed every old lady's lawn in the neighborhood. I looked for pennies and nickels wedged in the crack of the car seat or under the cushions of the couch. I even sold my yo-yo to Mel Farris. When I gathered together all the money I could, I put it in a paper bag and set out on a mission to buy my momma a birthday ring.

I'm sure she knew what I was doing. She probably figured it out when I measured her finger four times and asked her sneaky questions about birthstones. My bicycle took me across town to the big stores. It was a lot harder than I thought it would be. There were different sizes and colors and the price tags made me wonder what a person would have to do for so much money.

At the jewelry store down by the square I went inside and held my face up against the glass case staring at glittering jewelry. I looked up to see my mother standing at the window outside smiling in at me. I walked out to see her.

"Mom." She was still smiling.

"Yes."

"Could you drive me to the store outside of town by

the football field? I'm not allowed to go that far on my bike."

"O.K." she said, "Let's go for a ride."

We rode silently. When my mother wasn't looking I wadded up the brown paper bag and shoved it in my pocket. I covered the bulge with my hand.

"What's today, Mom?"

"Monday. School starts back in two weeks."

When we got to the store by the football field I asked my mom to wait in the car. This was my last chance. Her birthday was the next day, and I'd been to every store in town and looked at every stupid ring I could find. Either they didn't look like Mrs. Kendall's ring, or they cost more than all the money in my little brown bag.

My mother waited patiently in the car. The man behind the counter watched me slide slowly down the long glass case.

"What can I do ya for, young man?"

I pulled out my paper sack and sat it on the counter.

"My momma's birthday is tomorrow. I saved up money cuttin' yards and stuff. I wanna get her a ring. A pretty ring."

The man unraveled the paper sack and counted my money.

He said, "Sorry, young man, but you don't have enough money for any of the rings in my store. Maybe you could go across the street to the drugstore and get your momma something like chocolate candy or maybe some flowers."

I grabbed my bag from the counter top and ran outside. I could see my mother across the parking lot with the windows down. She watched me every step of the walk from the store to the car door. I felt like I would die. When I got inside the car and pulled the heavy door closed she smiled at me.

"What's the matter, baby?"

I started to cry. "Momma, I wanted to get you a ring like Mrs. Kendall's for your birthday. I saved my money, cut Mrs. Peterson's yard, and sold my yo-yo. I went to every store in town. This was the last store, Momma, and I can't get you a ring. I don't have enough money, and I know daddy won't get you nothin'. He'll forget again. I know he will."

My momma scooted over on the seat and put her arm around me. She said, "Baby, you've already given me my present."

I didn't understand.

She said, "I have a boy that loves me so much he saved his money, and sold his yo-yo, cut the neighbors' yards, and rode all around town on his bike to find a ring for his mother. Nobody's ever done that for me. Nobody."

●

In my years of keeping the God file I have come to believe that the greatest evidence I have found of God's existence is not me, but is the search itself. I have to believe that God sent me on this search, and the search itself has nourished and sustained me. It is the most obvious gift from God, and it has been right in front of me every single day.

While the effort of the search gave me daily sustenance, it has also led to an end, an understanding. Through this search I have found myself by finding my mother, my father, pieces of my brother, and so many other people and ideas. I have to give credit to my mother's religion for helping steer me in the direction I've traveled. Although I cannot believe each and every teaching of the Catholic Church, it provided to me a foundation and curiosity I may not have had otherwise. At the start, my point of beginning seemed only a tick away from another man's beginning, but twenty-two years later I have ended up in a place faraway.

In Catholicism we were taught to believe that there is a hierarchy in the closeness to God. But at this moment, this exact moment, no one could be closer to God than I am. I can close my eyes and feel His arm around me, tight and sure, like I was a little boy again.

afterward

My name is John Coleman. I am the one who found Gabriel that morning in his cell. His face was blue, and I knew immediately he was dead. I recognized the little foil pill wrappers clutched in his hand. I watched the guards carry him away and clean out his cell like he never existed.

Gabriel was my friend, if a man can have a friend in a place like prison. He was a decent man. For as long as I knew him, Gabriel kept a box under his bed. I never asked him about it. On the day that he died I found Gabriel's box under my own bed. I don't know how he managed to put it there, or when, but I do know why. It was Gabriel's gift to me.

Not long after that day I was finally released on parole. Gabriel's file was full of notes, and pictures, and smaller files with titles written on the top. He had done all the work for me. The important pieces were put together in a separate file inside the box. There's no way for me to know the chronological order because there were no dates except on the copies of letters to Janie. I am not sure whether Gabriel wrote the section entitled rage or whether he copied it from a book. If it was copied, I apologize to the author.

Between odd jobs, the best a convicted felon can do, I read through Gabriel's file. It slowly began to come together. It has helped me understand myself in much the same way I think it helped Gabriel understand himself and the people in his life. There are messages I find in his writings, between the sentences and inside the stories, that I carry with me. Most people in this world do not find themselves in a situation such as Gabriel's. We simply do not have the time, or take the time, to explore the little details. But when a person is in prison, especially a person like Gabriel Black, all he has are the little details to explore. Gabriel didn't have the opportunity to get lost in all the happiness and complications of children, marriages, careers, money, possessions, and freedom.

I found a page in the file entitled Faith. I believe it was the last thing Gabriel Black ever wrote, and I hope it was the way he felt when he died. I have a copy in my pocket, and I read it every day. I miss Gabriel. I miss our conversations. The world is a lesser place without him.

John Edward Coleman

Faith

And then I died.

A cool rush and silence. Complete silence. Suspended above nothing. A sense of being part of everything, without a body, skin, to hold me in. The knowledge that something strange and wonderful will happen soon, without the anxiety of the unknown. I can feel my father's hand in mine as we walk across the field together. I can actually feel the warmth of his hand.

A slow light begins, soft and gradually building, with no sense of seeing, just feeling. And with the light there is a warmth. Surrounding. My mother is close. It occurs to me that I am in a womb, floating in the warm fluid, eyes closed, safe, touching with tiny hands, unafraid.

And I begin to move. Gently, pulled towards the soft white light. Pulled by the strings of faith. Tiny, unbreakable strings connecting me to the light, wrapped in trust. And suddenly there is a sense of leaving something behind, somebody, as the light grows brighter. And a perfect hand reaches to me. Maybe the hand of the Father, or Jesus, or my mother who lifts me in the cool air.

And I am born unto myself.

My faith now self-contained, beyond the point of viability. It will survive the holocaust of eternal nothingness, the indifference of damnation, or endless peace, whichever comes first, or never comes at all.

I am a man.

Proud. Unsure. Prepared and hopeful. Like a baby standing for my first step.

May it be so.

Gabriel Black

About the Author

Frank Turner Hollon was born in 1963 in Huntsville, Alabama, and raised in Slidell, Louisiana. He graduated from Louisiana Tech University in 1985 and Tulane Law School in 1988. Frank lives in Baldwin County, Alabama, with his wife Allison and their children and practices law at Hoiles, Dasinger & Hollon in Robertsdale. He has four published novels, *The Pains of April*, *The God File*, *A Thin Difference*, and *Life is a Strange Place*. Frank's short stories have appeared in *Stories from the Blue Moon Café, Volumes I* and *II*.

Acknowledgments

The journey from the written word to an actual book takes a great deal of support and effort from other people. Those people include my dad and Virginia, mom and Skip, Allison, Smokey Davis, Kevin Shannon, Mike Strecker, Kyle Jennings, Robert Bell, Kip Howard, Barry Munday, Sharon Hoiles, Mike Dasinger, Melissa Bass, David Poindexter, Kate Nitze, and of course, Pat Walsh and my friend Sonny Brewer.